REVENGE OF THE INVISIBLE BOY

GOOSEBUMPS®

Also available as ebooks

ALSO AVAILABLE:

REVENGE OF THE
INVISIBLE BOY

R.L. STINE

SCHOLASTIC INC.

Goosebumps book series created by Parachute Press, Inc.
Copyright © 2019 by Scholastic Inc.

ISBN 978-1-338-35571-0

10 9 8 7 6 5 4 3 2 1   19 20 21 22 23

Printed in the U.S.A.   40
First printing 2019

SLAPPY HERE, EVERYONE.

Welcome to My World.

Yes, it's *SlappyWorld*—you're only *screaming* in it! Hahaha!

It's such a shame people don't have words to describe me. I mean, words like *brilliant* and *talented* and *good-looking* don't really do it, do they? But go ahead. Feel free to use them anyway! Hahaha.

Do you know how smart I am?

Of *course* you don't.

I'm so smart, the dictionary asked me to define it. Ha.

Some people say I'm evil. That's ridiculous. Does it mean I'm evil just because I do horrible things day and night? No way!

Actually, I'm a nice guy. Know how nice I am? Last week, I rescued a bird that had fallen out of a tree. I carefully picked it up and carried it home.

It was delicious! Hahaha!

Well, I have a story for you, and naturally, it's a *scary* story. The story is told by a boy named Frankie Miller. Frankie and his friends are really into magic. They love to watch magicians and perform tricks.

Frankie is about to learn just how dangerous some magic tricks can be.

Want to get a head start on the story? Start screaming *now*! Hahaha!

I call the story *Revenge of the Invisible Boy*.

It's just one more terrifying tale from *SlappyWorld*.

Have I mentioned that I hate Ari Goodwyn?

I guess I haven't mentioned it since I'm just starting my story.

But I hate Ari, and you'll soon see why.

My name is Frankie Miller. I'm twelve. My magician name is Magic Miller. My story starts while I'm onstage in the auditorium in front of everyone at Han Solo Middle School in Barberton, Ohio.

As you can probably tell, I like to be serious and careful and accurate and correct. Those are all important for a magician—especially for a magician who is just learning how to do dangerous tricks.

I'm in a magic club with my friends Melody Richmond and Eduardo Martinez. And Ari. One reason I hate Ari Goodwyn is that he is *not* serious and careful. And there are two other things. Ari is a goof. And he's a flake. And there's no place for a goof or a flake when you are performing magic.

Our magic club meets every Wednesday after school. We study the history of magic. We read about all the great magicians of the past. And we learn how to perform new tricks.

We don't really want Ari in our club. He makes fun of us. He messes up our tricks. He has no interest in the history of magic. He has a bad attitude. And *that's* the best thing I can say about him.

The problem is, the rec room in Ari's basement is the only place we can meet. It's the only place that's big enough for us to spread out and try new tricks.

Also, Ari's mom makes the best chocolate chip cookies and the sweetest lemonade. She brings them downstairs for us every week and then goes back upstairs and leaves us alone.

So, what choice do we have?

We have to keep Ari in the club—even though we wish he'd go upstairs with his mother and leave us alone, too.

Anyway ...

As my story starts, I'm onstage in the auditorium. Mrs. Hazy, our principal, has introduced me as Magic Miller. And I am about to perform the most difficult illusion I know.

I am about to levitate myself off the floor.

I'm going to appear to float and hang suspended six feet in the air.

Of course, it's an illusion. I can't really float off the floor. I admit I have tried it several times

4

when no one was watching. But I quickly learned the hard truth. I don't have any special powers.

Everything I do has to be a trick, an illusion.

Some nights I dream that I can fly. In the dream, Melody, Eduardo, and I are performing a magic act onstage. We are wearing long red capes and holding magic wands. And as we end the act, our capes rise up behind us. We raise our wands in front of us. And we fly off the stage and out of the auditorium.

The dream is so real, I think I can feel the cool wind on my face. The three of us fly—like superheroes—across the starry night sky.

I'm always so disappointed when I wake up.

As I said, I'm a serious, sensible guy. So I'm always surprised when my dreams are so wild, so unrealistic.

Anyway . . .

I'm about to amaze everyone in my school by levitating above the stage.

It took a long time to set up the illusion properly.

I have a harness strapped to my back that no one can see. The curtain behind me is black. And I have a strong black cord that stretches up from my harness. No one can see the cord because it matches the curtain.

There is a catwalk above the stage. It's like a metal scaffold with a wide walkway. The catwalk is hidden by the curtain.

So no one in the audience can see that Ari is

5

high above me. He is kneeling at the top of the catwalk.

The black cord stretches from my harness up to the catwalk. Up there, it is coiled around a big metal wheel. You know, the kind of wheel you wrap a garden hose around.

When Ari turns the wheel, the cord will go tight. And then, as he turns it more, the cord will lift me off the floor. It will look as if I am floating up on my own.

Ari will pull me up at least six feet off the floor. All he has to do is hold on to the wheel. Hold it steady so I appear to float. Then he will lower me slowly to the floor as the audience claps and cheers and goes wild.

It was hard to set up. But an easy illusion to perform.

Melody and Eduardo were watching me from the side of the stage. Melody flashed me a thumbs-up.

I stepped into place. I could feel the cord tugging at the harness hidden on my back. I made my announcement to the audience:

"I will now perform the levitation trick known to only a few magicians in history," I shouted. "Watch carefully. Without any props or devices, I will rise up from the stage and float in midair. Don't try this at home, kids!"

I thought that was a pretty good joke. But only a few kids laughed.

6

I took a deep breath and raised my right hand. That was the signal for Ari to start pulling me up.

I felt the cord jerk. Then a hard tug.

And yes. Yes. The cord pulled me up. I stood straight with my hands out to my sides.

I heard a few kids gasp as my shoes left the stage floor.

Higher. A few inches off the floor.

I heard shouts in the audience. A few more gasps. Some kids started to clap.

The cord tugged hard as I rose. Two feet off the floor now. Slowly floating higher. Higher. Three feet. More.

A hush fell over the auditorium. I glimpsed Melody and Eduardo smiling at me from the wings.

I raised my right hand again. Ari followed my signal. He held tight, allowing me to float in place for a moment. I was at least four or five feet off the floor. One or two more feet to go.

The audience started to clap. I took a short bow with my head. My shoes dangled in midair.

And then . . .

I felt something go wrong.

Was the cord loosening?

Yes.

My breath caught in my throat as I felt myself start to go down. Fast.

And I opened my mouth in a frightened scream: "NOOOOOO! HELLLLLP!"

7

2

My scream cut off as I landed hard on my belly. My breath whooshed out of my open mouth. I sprawled there, choking, struggling to breathe.

On the catwalk above me, I heard Ari. "Ooops. My bad."

I knew what had happened. The wheel handle had slipped out of his hands. Or else he had just let it go.

"My bad!" he shouted. "Sorry, Frankie. Seriously. I'm sorry."

Still gasping for breath, I glanced up. Ari had a grin on his face. He wasn't sorry. Who makes an apology with a grin on his face?

Melody and Eduardo hurried across the stage. They took my arms and helped me to my feet. Then they guided me to the wings.

The audience was silent. I heard a few boos.

"He ruined the trick. He made me look like a loser," I muttered, shaking my head.

"Ari strikes again," Melody said.

"He embarrassed me in front of the whole school." I finally started to breathe normally. I gazed at Eduardo and Melody. "Do you think it was an accident?"

"It had to be," Eduardo said. "Ari is a creep. But he wouldn't try to hurt you."

Eduardo is a nice guy, and he always wants to think nice things about people. Sometimes he's so cheerful and kind, it gets on my nerves.

"After he dropped you, I saw him grinning," Melody said. "Like it was a big joke."

"That's because he was embarrassed," Eduardo insisted. "He knew he messed up. What did you expect Ari to do, Melody? Burst into tears?"

"He didn't have to grin," she replied. "He grins every time he messes up. How about last week when we performed for our first kids' birthday party? He forgot to load the flowers into our magic wands, and we stood there waving them like idiots."

"He just forgot," Eduardo said.

"But then Ari wrapped his cape around that little boy's head and scared him to death. And the birthday boy's mother asked us to leave."

"She overreacted," Eduardo said.

"How can you stick up for him?" Melody demanded, giving Eduardo a hard shove. "He messes up everything."

Eduardo shrugged. He didn't answer.

I rubbed my chest. My ribs were sore from the fall. "Did I ever mention that I hate him?" I said. "I wish there was some way to pay him back."

Melody nodded. "Yeah. I wish."

3

Melody set a tall glass pitcher filled with water down on the coffee table. "I'm going to show you an awesome new trick," she said. "My uncle Clyde taught it to me."

"I thought your uncle Clyde is a barber," I said.

She nodded. "He is. But he does magic tricks on the side. You know. It's his hobby."

Ari laughed. "Like he cuts off your ear, then magically puts it back."

Eduardo grinned. "I'd like to see that trick."

The four of us were in Ari's basement for our weekly Magic Club meeting. Mrs. Goodwyn had already served the cookies and lemonade. Now we were sitting around the low coffee table in the middle of the rec room, settling down to business.

Buster, Ari's big dog, was nosing around under the food table, searching for cookie crumbs that might have dropped to the floor. I'm not a dog person. To be totally honest, I'm a little afraid of them.

11

Buster must sense that. Which explains why he spends most of his time pestering me. He likes to leap on me and poke me with his huge head and lick me till my skin drips with his sticky saliva.

Dogs know when you're not a dog person. And then they always pick you out for special treatment.

I've begged Ari several times to shut his dog upstairs. But he says that will hurt Buster's feelings. *My* feelings, of course, don't count.

Melody likes to throw her arms around Buster's chest and give him long hugs. But the big creature pretty much ignores her. He only has eyes for me.

I leaned forward on the green leather couch and watched Melody arrange the tall water pitcher. Ari stood behind the couch.

Eduardo slid off his chair and dropped to his knees at the side of the table. He ran a hand back through his straight black hair. "Are you going to pour this on somebody?"

"Of course not," Melody said. "It's a really good trick." She raised her eyes to me. "I need your baseball cap. Get it for me."

"Huh?" I gasped. "What are you going to do? That's my best Yankees cap. Dad got it for me last time my family visited New York."

"Don't worry about it. Just go get it," Melody snapped. When she's showing off a new trick, she can get pretty intense.

Melody has red hair. And she's tiny. I think

she's the smallest person in our class. But she's also definitely the boldest.

I've never seen her back down from an argument. And she usually wins. And she's a terror on the soccer field. At least, that's what other kids on the team tell me.

I crossed the rec room and pulled my Yankees cap from my jacket pocket. Then Melody took it from me. She placed it upside down next to the pitcher of water.

I dropped back onto the couch. "What are you going to do? Are you going to pour the water into my cap?"

Melody nodded. "You've seen this trick?"

"I've never seen it," Eduardo said.

"Can't wait to see Frankie's cap get soaked," Ari chimed in.

Melody frowned at him. "That's not going to happen. I'm going to pour the pitcher of water into Frankie's cap. And when I lift the cap into the air, it will be perfectly dry."

Ari rolled his eyes. "I'm laughing already." He slapped the back of my head from behind. "Good luck getting a new Yankees cap, dude."

"No worries," Melody said. "This trick never fails."

I gritted my teeth. Was my cap really going to end up perfectly dry?

Melody reached for the handle of the water pitcher.

But before she could lift the pitcher off the table, I heard the *thud* of heavy footsteps. I looked up in time to see Buster rear back on his hind legs—and *leap* onto the table.

He banged the pitcher hard with his big head. It toppled over and shattered. Shards of glass flew off the tabletop. And the water splashed in a tall wave into my baseball cap.

My cap was soaked through. I made a grab for it. But Buster shoved it to the floor with a big paw.

"Noooooo." I pulled the drenched cap from the floor and brushed off shards of broken glass.

Buster dove for it. I tried to jump to my feet. But before I could move, he leaped into my lap. His fat tongue came out and he began ferociously licking my face.

"Get him off! Get him off!" I cried. I tried to push him away with both hands. But he weighed two tons, and he was enjoying the taste of my face too much to budge.

"Don't push him away," Ari said. "He'll feel rejected."

Rejected?

Finally, Eduardo tempted Buster with a dog biscuit, and the hulking beast climbed down from my lap.

Ari slapped the back of my head again. "Buster likes you, Frankie. Weird, huh?"

I spun around, ready to punch out Ari's lights. But I'm not a violent person. I think a lot about what I'd like to do to Ari. But I would never do any of it. Partly because it would be wrong. And partly because I'm a bit of a coward. I mean, I'm not a fighter. I'm a sensible, civilized guy.

Buster enjoyed his cookie. He sat down in the corner, probably to celebrate his total victory over me.

We cleaned up the broken glass. Then we sat around the table and tried to restart our meeting. "I don't want to go over the whole thing again," I said. "But the levitation performance was a horrible disaster."

"I already apologized," Ari said. "Can I help it if my hand slipped?"

"Yes, you can," I snapped.

"I lost focus for a second," he said. "It could happen to anyone."

Should I hit him now?

"Did you see Morgan Traub's Instagram of me on the stage floor?" I asked. "She called me Frankie Fall-Down."

"Derek Otis posted one, too," Ari said. "He called you Frankie Face-First! Haha."

I sighed. "I'm a joke. Thanks to you, Ari, I'm a joke. Seriously. Kids look at me in the halls, and they burst out laughing."

"Those kids are just being mean," Melody said, adjusting her single braid from one side to the other. "Everyone knows accidents happen. You're not a joke, Frankie."

"Kids will forget," Ari said. "You'll only be a joke for a few more months at the most. Maybe till the end of the semester."

I squinted at him. "Is that supposed to make me feel better?"

"Not really," he said, and grinned that hateful grin again.

"We have to stop talking about it," Eduardo said. "We have to do another show to prove we're not failures."

"We should stick to card tricks," Melody said. "They're a lot easier. And you can't break any bones doing card tricks."

"You could snap your wrist," Ari said.

Everyone ignored him.

"Card tricks aren't good onstage," I said. "The audience is too far away to see anything."

Ari poked me in the side. "Get up. I'll show you a good trick we can do."

"Huh?" I gazed at him. "What kind of trick?"

"Come here. I'll show you," he said. He pulled me to my feet. Then he led me across the room to his dad's exercise equipment. "Frankie, grab the bar up there."

I hesitated. "That bar? Why?"

"My dad does fifty chin-ups on it every morning," Ari said. "But you don't have to do any lifts. I'm going to show you a good trick. Grab the bar."

I glanced back. Melody and Eduardo hadn't moved. They were watching from across the room.

16

I decided to play along. Maybe Ari really did have a good trick.

I stood on tiptoes, reached high, and grabbed the metal bar with both hands. "Now what?"

"Just hold on to the bar," Ari said. "Grip it tightly. Don't let go. This is a good trick. You'll see."

My arms were stretched as high as they would go. My head tilted back, I gripped the bar tightly in both hands.

And Ari tugged my jeans down to my ankles.

I uttered a startled cry.

Ari backed away, laughing like a hyena.

I heard Melody and Eduardo laughing, too.

And, of course, today I'd worn the SpongeBob boxer shorts my grandmother gave me. Not too embarrassing.

I quickly pulled my jeans up. But their laughter continued, ringing off the low basement ceiling.

I knew my face was bright red. But I didn't care. I had only one thought in mind: *How will I pay Ari back?*

Strangely enough, the answer came to me one week later.

We didn't have time for complaints or arguments or dumb tricks at our next Magic Club meeting. We were too excited.

We only wanted to talk about Mystical Marvin.

Yes. Mystical Marvin. Maybe the most famous, most legendary magician in the entire world was coming to our town. He was performing at the Town Center.

My dad is on the Barberton town council. And he got us four tickets in the second row of the theater.

It was the most awesome thing my dad ever did, and he knew it. When he showed us the tickets, the grin wouldn't leave his face. I think it stayed there for *days*!

Melody, Eduardo, and I couldn't believe we could be so lucky. Of course, Ari acted as if he didn't know what the fuss was about.

I was so happy, I let Buster lick my face when

we met in Ari's basement. I didn't even try to push the big beast away. Just let him slobber all over.

"Did you read the Wikipedia page about Mystical Marvin?" Melody asked. "It says he has all kinds of powers that scientists have been unable to explain."

"He's a master magician," Eduardo said. "I've read everything about him, and I watched some YouTube videos."

"He says he doesn't do tricks," I added. "He says everything he does is real."

"And you believe that?" Ari said, shaking his head. "Do you believe in the Easter Bunny, too?"

"Whoa. Hold on, Ari—" I started.

"Mystical Marvin does tricks like everyone else," Ari insisted. "Maybe he's slicker than other dudes. But he still does tricks."

"Not true," I said. "Why do you always have to tear everyone down?"

Ari shrugged. "I'm not tearing him down. I'm just saying he's a magician. That's all. And magicians do tricks."

"He's more like a wizard than a magician," Eduardo said. "I think a lot of his illusions go back hundreds of years to when there were real sorcerers in Europe."

Ari rolled his eyes. "For sure."

"Can we stop arguing?" I said. "All I know is, his show is going to be seriously unbelievable.

And we'll be sitting so close, we'll practically be in his act!"

And sure enough, that night, there we were. My dad dropped the four of us off at the show. We made our way down the crowded aisle and found our seats in the big auditorium. Second row, right in the center!

I could barely sit still. No joke. I don't think I'd ever been this excited. Even when my dad took me to my first baseball game at Yankee Stadium in New York.

I gazed at the red curtain across the stage. A white spotlight darted back and forth over it. Melody poked my shoulder. "Didn't you hear me? I've been calling your name."

"Sorry," I said. "I . . . was thinking about Mystical Marvin."

"Do you think he'll do the water tank trick?" she asked. "You know. The one where he stays underwater for nearly half an hour without breathing? I want to see that close-up. Maybe we can figure out how he does it."

"Maybe," I said. "But I don't think so. I think he just taught himself to hold his breath for half an hour."

"Yeah. Maybe he had his lungs enlarged," Ari said. Then he laughed.

The lights dimmed. I gripped the arms of my seat. My heart was pounding. The audience grew silent. A man's voice on the loudspeakers told us to silence our cell phones.

And then, in an explosion of flashing lights brighter than the sun, Mystical Marvin came trotting onto the stage.

5

The applause roared down the theater like an ocean wave. Still blinking from the lingering flashes of light in my eyes, I felt as if I was being swept up. Lifted from my seat and carried to the stage on the rise and fall of the wild applause.

Just my excitement, I guess.

I gripped the seat back in front of me and leaned forward to get a good look at Mystical Marvin. I was only a few feet away from him!

Mystical Marvin swept back the satiny red cape he was wearing. He raised both hands, and the crowd began to settle down. The spotlight made his blue eyes sparkle. He had ringlets of blond curls down to his shoulders. Under the shiny red cape, he wore a white tuxedo so bright, it practically glowed.

"Good evening, friends!" he shouted in a deep voice. "Welcome to my world of sorcery." He raised his right hand, snapped his fingers—and disappeared in a burst of light.

I turned to Melody. "How did he do that? Where is he?"

Melody shrugged. "Maybe there's a trapdoor in the stage?"

"We would have seen it," I said.

A round yellow spotlight suddenly swept over the balcony high above the stage. I turned and saw Mystical Marvin sitting up there in the first row. He stood up and took a bow.

"True magic can take you many places," he called down. "Even from a stage to the balcony."

The balcony light went dark. Two seconds later, Mystical Marvin came strutting back across the stage. The audience burst into loud applause.

Ari leaned over and shouted in my ear. "I know how he does it," he said. "It's easy."

"How?" I said. "How does he do it?"

"He's twins." Ari slapped my shoulder. "He has a twin brother."

I frowned at him. "I don't think so."

I turned back to the stage. The curtain slid open. Behind it stood a wide cave painted on a backdrop. It looked deep and dark. A sign above it read: SORCERER'S CAVE.

Next to the cave stood a tall glass tank, filled with water.

"He *is* doing the water tank trick!" I exclaimed to Melody.

"Now we'll see how he breathes when he's underwater," Eduardo said.

Even though the cave was just a painting, somehow Mystical Marvin walked right into the painted opening. When he stepped back out, he announced his levitation trick. "The trick of levitation has been shrouded in secrecy for decades. I was unable to unlock the secret. So I created my own method of floating in midair."

He stepped to the front of the stage. I could have leaned over the seat in front of me and touched him. That's how close I was.

"I use no ropes or hidden cords," he announced. "I have nothing attached to me, nothing to pull me up from the floor. But watch my feet. My levitation powers begin with my feet. And then they allow my entire body to float. Watch carefully."

He backed up until he stood in front of the painted cave opening. He lowered his hands to his sides and stood very stiff and straight.

"Concentration is the key," he said. "Everybody, concentrate. Concentrate . . ."

The auditorium fell silent. I think everyone was staring at the shiny black boots on Mystical Marvin's feet.

"Concentrate . . ." he repeated, as if hypnotizing the audience. "Everybody concentrate . . ."

And his boots lifted off the stage floor. An inch . . . two inches . . . then higher.

He kept his body stiff and straight. Arms down at his sides. And he floated off the floor, into the air. In seconds, he was at least four or five feet off the floor.

The waves of applause came down the rows of seats. Mystical Marvin nodded but didn't change his erect position.

Ari slapped my shoulder again. "Big whoop," he said, shouting in my ear. "He's using a harness, too. Do you see it?"

I shoved him away. "No. I don't see it. He's not using a harness. He has no strings attached or anything."

"Know what you need? You need glasses," Ari said.

Mystical Marvin came floating back down to the stage floor, greeted by another explosion of applause.

He did the water tank trick next. He changed into a wet suit and started to lower himself into the tank from the top. "I will try to set the world record tonight for staying underwater—and living!" he announced, his head still above the water. "When I am totally underwater, watch my lips carefully. You will see that no air bubbles escape. I will not breathe until I pull myself from the tank."

He signaled to his assistant. She stepped out from the wings, a young woman with curly brown hair, wearing a sparkly evening gown.

She carried a big square panel of glass in front

of her. The tank lid. Mystical Marvin signaled again, and she placed the lid over the tank.

Then she brought out a large, round clock on a pedestal. She set it up beside the tank and started it up. It began counting off the seconds.

Mystical Marvin sucked in a long, deep breath. He lowered himself, letting himself sink until his feet were on the bottom. Then he stood there, facing the audience.

My eyes kept going from Mystical Marvin to the clock at the side of the tank. Five minutes . . . Ten . . .

Music played. Lights flashed. The audience didn't move.

Mystical Marvin jumped up and down and made swimming motions with his arms. But he didn't come up for air. And no air bubbles escaped his lips.

Ari leaned over me again. "I know how he does it."

"No, you don't," I said. "We couldn't be any closer, and there's still no way to figure it out."

"He's not in the tank," Ari said. "He's standing *behind* the tank. He isn't inside it. It only looks like he's in there."

"Ari, give me a break," I said. "Look at him. He's floating and swimming in there. He's definitely underwater."

"Keep watching," Ari insisted. "He isn't in the tank."

I shoved Ari away. "Stop trying to ruin this for me," I said angrily. "You've tried to ruin every trick. You don't know anything about magic. So shut up and let me enjoy the show."

He stuck out his bottom lip and made a pouty face. Like I hurt his feelings. Then he laughed.

I don't think he has any feelings.

But at least I shut him up for a while.

Mystical Marvin stayed underwater for exactly twenty-five minutes. Then he signaled to his assistant to remove the lid.

He burst up from the tank, gasping for air. He choked and wheezed and hoisted himself to the floor, dripping a puddle of water around him.

"Guess he *was* in the tank," I said to Ari. "He sure looks wet."

Ari shrugged and didn't reply.

When the applause died down, Mystical Marvin said: "That trick was taught to me by a scientist who studied the oceans for many years. He taught himself to swim underwater for longer and longer stretches. Eventually, he became like an aquatic animal, like a seal or a walrus. He could stay underwater as long as he liked."

Mystical Marvin wiped water from his long, curly blond hair. "And now I am the only man on earth who can match that scientist. I, too, am an aquatic animal."

"See? It's not a trick," I whispered to Ari.

He rolled his eyes. "You're so dumb."

Mystical Marvin trotted off the stage as music came up and the colored spotlights danced over the set again. He returned—in seconds—wearing his white tuxedo and red satin cape.

He stepped to the front of the stage. "Here's something I always enjoy," he said, sweeping the cape back. "I'm going to make one of you disappear tonight."

The theater filled with murmurs and some laughter and a few cries of surprise.

"This is real," Mystical Marvin said. "It isn't a trick. It isn't an illusion. I'm going to choose one of you to *really* disappear—maybe *forever*!"

More murmurs and whispers.

He stepped to the very edge of the stage. Lights from the stage floor made his face glow red and his blond hair shimmer.

"Let's see . . ." he said, rubbing his chin and staring down at the first few rows of seats. "Who will disappear tonight? Who shall I choose?"

And then his hand shot out—and he pointed his finger right at *me*.

"How about *you*, young man?"

I thought my heart was going to leap right through my shirt!

He isn't pointing at me. Or is he? Is he really pointing at me?

"You. Young fella. Get up here!" Mystical Marvin insisted.

My legs were wobbly. Like rubber bands. But

somehow I climbed to my feet. My friends were laughing. I guess they saw how *terrified* I was.

I'm going onstage with Mystical Marvin!

I stumbled over Melody and Eduardo and squeezed down the long row of seats into the aisle. Mystical Marvin pointed to the wooden stairs at the side of the stage. Somehow I made my way up them.

And there I was, trembling next to him, the stage lights completely blinding me. My heart raced so hard, I could barely breathe.

Mystical Marvin pulled me close to him. He pointed down to the second row of seats I had just come from.

"Say good-bye to your friends," he said. "You're going on a long journey."

His red cape flashed in front of my eyes. His blue eyes appeared even brighter this close to them, as if they were electric. He narrowed them at me as he kept his hand on my shoulder.

"What's your name?" I heard his voice, and I heard the echo of his voice as it traveled over the theater.

I was so nervous, I had to think. *My name?*

"Frankie Miller," I finally managed to say. And then, I blurted out, "I'm a magician, too."

That made the audience laugh.

Mystical Marvin's eyes flashed. A smile crossed his face. "You're a magician, too? What kind of magic do you do, Frankie?"

Again, I had to think. My brain had turned to marshmallow.

"All kinds," I said finally.

He nodded. The blue eyes . . . the shining waterfall of blond hair . . . his grinning face . . . It didn't seem real. He was like an illusion floating inside the red cape.

"Frankie, do you ever do disappearing tricks?" he asked.

"N-no," I stammered. "Those tricks are hard."

The audience laughed again. The laughter seemed miles away.

"Yes, they are," Mystical Marvin agreed. "And when other magicians vanish in plain sight, it's just a trick. Just an illusion. But . . . when I vanish in plain sight . . . When I disappear in a flash in front of an audience, it's *real*, Frankie."

He removed his hand from my shoulder and took a step back. The cape billowed behind him.

"And tonight, I'm going to show you how to disappear," he continued. "And it isn't a trick, Frankie."

He raised his voice so the audience could hear every word. "You will really disappear. Later, you will appear again. I hope it's soon. But I can't guarantee it. I can't predict when you will return."

I swallowed. "You mean—?"

"I have performed this many times," Mystical Marvin said. "On many victims. Most times, the victim returns in less than a week."

A week?

A hard shudder shook my body. "But . . . my parents—" I choked out.

Mystical Marvin raised a hand to silence

me. "You will go to a world unknown by most humans on earth," he said. "Another world, a hidden world, Frankie. Maybe you won't even *want* to return from there."

"B-but—" I stammered.

He placed a hand over my head. "Prepare yourself." He leaned toward me. "Do you have any last words?"

"Excuse me?" I cried. "You mean—"

"Any last words before you disappear?"

Another shudder shook my body. "Well... uh ... good-bye, I guess."

The audience didn't laugh. The theater was silent. I guessed everyone knew they were about to watch a serious moment.

"When I tap your head twice, you will disappear, Frankie," Mystical Marvin said. "Ready? One ..." He tapped the top of my head.

I shut my eyes. I gritted my teeth.

I waited for the second tap. But it didn't come.

When I opened my eyes, Mystical Marvin had stepped back. He was grinning at me.

"Hey, Frankie—I was just messing with you," he said. "Did I give you a scare?"

"Yes," I choked out. "You did."

"Well, you had a close call. But I'm not going to make you disappear after all." Still grinning, he shook my hand. "Nice to meet another magician. Go back and take your seat." He motioned to the audience. "Give Frankie some love, everyone!"

I hurried back to my seat on trembling legs as the audience clapped for me. Eduardo slapped me a high five as I sat down. Ari leaned forward and whispered, "I knew he wouldn't do it."

Mystical Marvin stepped to the front of the stage. "Frankie was a good sport," he said. He walked up to the bright spotlight.

"I'm not going to make Frankie disappear tonight," he said. "I'm going to make *myself* disappear. Good night, everyone. Thank you all, and good-bye."

He pulled a small bottle from under his cape. In the bright spotlight, a yellow liquid sparkled inside the bottle. Mystical Marvin tilted the bottle to his lips. He drank from the bottle—

—and vanished into thin air.

I stared, blinking at the empty stage. The yellow circle of light against the red curtain. Empty. Gone. Mystical Marvin had disappeared.

Silence in the theater. No one knew whether to applaud or not.

Was that it? Was the show over?

Yes. The stage lights flickered off. The auditorium lights came up. People stood up, grabbed their jackets, and started up the aisles to the exit.

"How did he disappear like that? With mirrors?"

"I think something backstage pulled him through the curtain."

"He's amazing. It's like he's not human."

"Did he really hold his breath for half an hour?"

Everyone seemed to be talking at once. People shrugged and shook their heads. No one had a clue how Mystical Marvin had done any of the stunts he performed.

My heart was still racing from my close call onstage. Mystical Marvin had played a joke on me, but I didn't care. I knew I'd never forget being on the same stage he was.

Ari and Eduardo walked up the aisle ahead of Melody and me. I knew that Ari's father was coming to pick them up.

I grabbed Melody's arm and held her back. "Don't go," I said. "We're going backstage."

Her mouth dropped open. "We're *what*?"

"Going backstage," I said. "I have to know how he disappears like that."

"He won't tell us," Melody said. "What makes you think he'll talk to us? We'll only get in trouble."

"Come on. We've got to try," I said. "What could happen?"

I spotted a narrow hallway at the side of the stage. It led to the back of the theater. I pulled Melody toward it.

A tall, dark-suited usher stood blocking the way. I waited until he moved up the aisle to help a woman with a cane. "Hurry. Let's go," I whispered.

Melody and I darted into the narrow passageway.

Behind us, the theater was emptying quickly. The house lights on the ceiling dimmed. A few voices lingered, but it was getting quiet.

We made our way quickly along the hall, past the stage. At the end, the hall opened to a wide backstage area.

I stopped and gazed around. I expected it to be busy back here, bustling with people who worked on the show. But it was nearly silent.

An old man in a gray work uniform was down on his knees at the far wall. He was lifting stage props into a large chest. His head was down. He didn't see us.

Folding chairs were stacked against one wall. A tall stuffed penguin tilted beside them. A long rack of costumes stood against another wall. A spotlight lay on its back, dark, tilted toward the high ceiling. A stack of coiled black cords rose up beside it.

I listened for voices. The only sound was a loud, buzzing hum, probably the air conditioner.

"This is weird," I muttered.

Melody nodded. "Yeah. Where *is* everyone?" She tugged at her single braid with both hands. She does that when she's tense.

I was nervous, too. I knew we shouldn't be back here. And I knew Mystical Marvin probably would just tell us to go away.

But I had to try to talk to him.

I watched the worker in the gray uniform climb to his feet. He closed the lid to the chest and clicked it shut. Then he turned and disappeared into another back hall.

"Are we really all alone here?" I said to Melody. "Maybe we should go."

She gave me a little push. "We're here. We should try to find him."

Typical Melody. She doesn't scare easily, and she doesn't like to retreat.

I spotted a row of doors along the back wall. One of the doors was open and a light was on behind it.

"Those must be dressing rooms," Melody said. "Maybe that's Mystical Marvin's dressing room."

She cupped her hands around her mouth and shouted: "Mystical Marvin? Are you here?"

Silence.

I took a few steps, leading the way toward the open door. "Is anyone here?" I called. "Mystical Marvin? Anyone here?"

Silence.

I suddenly realized my hands were ice cold. I jammed them into my jeans pockets. Then I spun away from the dressing rooms and gazed all around the big backstage area.

No one around. Not even the guy in the gray uniform.

I turned and saw that Melody had crept up to the open dressing room door. She poked her head inside. Then she spun back to me. "No one here," she called. Her voice rang off the high concrete walls.

"Where did he go?" I asked.

"Maybe he runs out of the theater right after he disappears," she replied. "He didn't come back and take a bow or anything."

"You're probably right," I murmured. I couldn't hide my disappointment. I really wanted to meet Mystical Marvin and ask him about that disappearing trick.

Here we were . . . So close . . .

"Guess we should go," I said sadly.

Melody nodded. "Okay." She forced a smile. "We tried."

We both started toward the hall at the side. But we stopped when something pulsed in front of us. I blinked. What had I just seen?

Something strange. It seemed like the *air* had moved.

I stood close to Melody and we both stared straight ahead.

And it happened again. Some kind of shift in the air, as if the whole room had moved just a tiny bit. Just a shimmer. So quick.

It happened again. A fast, silent *pop* of air.

Then I jumped back as I saw a puff of smoke form in front of us. "Whoa. Check it out!" I cried.

The puff of white smoke lengthened until it resembled a fat snake, floating at eye level, so close in front of us. So close, I could touch it—if I wasn't terrified of what I was seeing.

The smoke coiled around itself as it floated. Twisted and bent. And grew larger. First, an oval-shaped cloud. Then spreading . . . spreading out until it rose in front of Melody and me as a curtain of white haze.

Melody and I both squinted into the bright white curtain.

And then . . . then it parted. The curtain opened from both sides.

And a scream escaped my throat: "I don't *believe* it!"

Mystical Marvin stepped forward, his red cape billowing behind him in the wall of mist. His blue eyes moved from Melody to me.

"You can believe it," he said. "It wasn't a trick. I really can go invisible."

I stood there blinking in amazement, my mouth hanging open.

Melody tugged at both sides of her hair. "You . . . You . . ." She was as speechless as I was.

"How long have you been here?" Mystical Marvin asked. "Why are you here? Everyone has gone."

He pulled off his cape, folded it in his hands, and set it down on top of the props chest. Then he shook his head hard, like a dog after a bath.

The wall of clouds had disappeared, but the air backstage still felt cold and damp.

"Melody and I . . . we wanted to meet you," I finally choked out.

He squinted at me. "You were onstage with me. Your name is Frankie?"

I nodded. "Frankie Miller." I stuck my hand out and he shook it.

I felt an electric charge go up my arm. *I'm shaking hands with Mystical Marvin.*

"This is my friend Melody Richmond," I said.

He shook hands with Melody, too.

Then he turned and strode toward the open dressing room. Melody and I hesitated for a moment. Then we followed him.

The room was small. A long mirror with lights all around it hung above a long counter. The counter had jars and bottles jammed over it. Probably stage makeup, I figured. A folding chair faced the mirror.

Mystical Marvin pulled off his white tuxedo bow tie and tossed it onto the dressing table. He unfastened the top button of his white shirt.

"Disappearing always makes me hungry," he said. "I'm going to run out and have an early dinner." He ran a comb through his blond ringlets.

Melody and I watched from the doorway. I didn't know if we were allowed into the room or not.

"We . . . have a magic club," I stammered.

Mystical Marvin set down the brush and turned to us. "Yes. You said onstage you were a magician."

I could feel my cheeks go red. "Well . . . I'm just learning. We're all really into magic."

"We try out new tricks," Melody said. "And we

do research on all the great magicians."

"Nice," he said. He tugged off his tuxedo jacket and hung it on a hook on the wall. "Of course, you realize I'm not a magician. I don't do tricks."

I took a deep breath. I needed courage to ask my next question. "I was wondering . . ." I started. "I mean, we're such huge fans. And . . . we're studying magic, and . . ."

He narrowed his eyes at me. "What are you trying to say, Frankie? Just go ahead and ask me."

"Can you tell us how you do the disappearing thing?" I blurted out breathlessly. "I mean . . . you could just give us a hint."

"We won't tell anyone," Melody added. "We swear."

He laughed. "Know what? You're both so serious, I'm going to show you. I'm going to show you the whole thing. But I have to remind you—it isn't a trick. No one else can do it, because I'm the only one who knows the formula."

Formula?

Melody and I exchanged glances. I don't think either one of us believed we were really standing in Mystical Marvin's dressing room. And he was really going to show us how he did one of his most incredible illusions.

He reached into the pocket of his tuxedo pants and pulled out a small bottle. He raised it so we could both see it clearly. It was full nearly to the top with a yellow liquid.

41

"That's the bottle you showed everyone onstage," I said.

He nodded. "Yes. This bottle contains the formula. The formula for disappearing. I was taught how to mix the formula by one of the last sorcerers in Europe."

"S-sorcerer?" I stammered.

"He was dying," Mystical Marvin said, holding the bottle in front of us. "And he didn't want the secret to die with him. I did many favors for him. I was his best student. And so he revealed the secret to me. He showed me how to mix the golden disappearing liquid."

Melody and I stared at the bottle as if hypnotized. Melody broke the silence: "What is it made of?"

"I can't reveal the details," Mystical Marvin said. "All I can tell you is, it's made from animal saliva. Amazing, huh? A truly amazing formula. One sip is all it takes. One sip and I go completely invisible."

My mind was whirring with questions. *Is he making this up? Is he playing a joke on us? Can he possibly be telling the truth?*

"Now you must excuse me," Mystical Marvin said. "I need to get changed and meet a friend at a restaurant." He shook hands with us again. "It was a pleasure—"

A shouted voice interrupted him. It must

have been the man we saw stuffing props into the trunk. "Marvin? Are you there? Phone call. Come pick it up."

Mystical Marvin brushed past us. "Excuse me. I have to take this," he said.

He hurried out the dressing room door. I listened to his running footsteps as he made his way toward the front of the theater.

"That was awesome!" Melody exclaimed. "It was like being in a dream or something. He actually explained how he does the disappearing thing."

She tapped my shoulder. "Frankie, are you in shock?"

I didn't answer her. I was looking for something.

I bent down and picked up an empty plastic water bottle from the floor.

"Frankie? Are we going?" Melody asked.

Again, I didn't answer. I set the empty plastic bottle down on the counter. Then I carefully . . . carefully . . . picked up Mystical Marvin's little bottle of yellow liquid.

Melody gasped. "What are you *doing*?"

My hand trembled as I removed the cap from the little formula bottle. Then I raised it and poured some into the empty water bottle. I didn't take a lot. Maybe two or three teaspoons.

I carefully closed both bottles. Then I hid the water bottle under my jacket. I gave Melody a little push toward the door. "Come on. Let's go."

"But—but—but—" she sputtered. "What did you just do?"

I glanced all around to make sure no one was around. Then I whispered, "I think I just figured out a way to pay Ari back."

I hid the bottle with the disappearing potion in my room at the bottom of my underwear drawer. It stressed me out to have it there. I checked to make sure it was okay several times a day.

Normally, I looked forward to our weekly Magic Club meetings. But now, every time I thought about our next meeting, my heart started to thump in my chest. I couldn't stop daydreaming about how awesome it would be when I put my revenge plan into action.

Ari . . . Poor Ari . . . You don't believe in magic? You have a big surprise in store for you.

Of course, Mom and Dad wanted to hear all about Mystical Marvin's performance. They both clapped their hands and cheered when I told them he had called me up onstage.

I didn't tell them that Melody and I had met him after the show. I was afraid I might blurt out something about taking the disappearing formula. Or what I planned to do with it.

I'm not the best secret-keeper in the world. I like to share. I guess that's why I enjoy performing magic tricks for people. But sometimes, I share too much.

Of course, I told Melody and Eduardo my plan. Melody had already guessed it. She thought it was the perfect revenge.

Eduardo had a million questions. Mainly, he wanted to know what would happen if Ari disappeared and didn't come back.

I laughed. "I guess we'd throw a party!" I said.

"No. Really," he insisted. "Aren't you afraid the whole idea may be dangerous?"

"Mystical Marvin disappeared and then came back ten minutes later," I reminded him. "He drank the same formula. So I don't think we need to worry."

"I think we *do* need to worry," Eduardo insisted. "What if Ari disappears and—"

"It didn't harm Mystical Marvin at all," I said. "One sip and he was invisible. A few minutes later, he was back and he was fine."

"But he's a pro," Eduardo said. "He's done it before. Lots of times. Maybe Ari won't know how to get back to normal."

"You're not going to talk me out of it," I said. "Ari has been asking for it ever since he joined our club. He even tried to ruin Mystical Marvin's show for me."

I was sorry I told Eduardo my plan. He's too

nice a guy. He worries about everyone, even Ari.

"If you want to stay home and skip the club meeting on Wednesday . . ." I started.

"Oh, no. No way," Eduardo replied. "Think I'd miss it? No way!"

So . . .

Wednesday after school, there we were. The four of us sat around the table in Ari's basement. Ari's mother brought down a big plate of banana cupcakes. Then she hurried upstairs to mix her famous lemonade.

Buster was licking the crumbs off my hands. Eduardo seemed a lot more quiet than usual. Melody kept glancing tensely at me and fiddling with her braid.

Of course, Ari decided to pick a fight about Mystical Marvin.

"He's a fake," Ari said. He had a smear of icing on his chin, but no one told him about it. "Other magicians have done his tricks. He stole his whole act."

I knew Ari was just trying to make me angry. But I couldn't hold back. I had to get into it with him.

"Have you done any research?" I demanded. "Have you read about other magicians who could levitate like that? Or stay underwater for half an hour?"

"Well . . ." Ari took a big bite of cupcake.

"Can you name another magician who does his disappearing trick?" I asked.

He chewed noisily. "I could just see his tricks were fake," he said. "You don't need to do research to see that. He had something behind him pulling him up off the floor. He didn't levitate."

"How come I couldn't see it?" I demanded.

Ari grinned. "I told you. Maybe you need glasses, Frankie."

"Let's stop arguing and try to have a meeting," Eduardo chimed in.

Before anyone else could say anything, Ari's mom came down the basement stairs carrying a tray in front of her. She had a pitcher of lemonade on the tray and four tall glasses already filled.

"Are you magicians having a nice discussion?" she asked.

"Yeah. Good," Ari answered. "But they're weird. They think magic is real. I just think it's a bunch of tricks."

"Maybe it's both," Mrs. Goodwyn said.

She placed a glass of lemonade in front of each of us. Then she tucked the tray under her arm and started up the stairs.

"Awesome cupcake, Mrs. Goodwyn," Eduardo called after her.

She turned around halfway up the stairs. "Thank you, Eduardo." She squinted at Buster, who was hunched by my chair, eyeing the rest of my cupcake. "Ari, do me a favor," she said. "Give Buster a quick walk, okay? He hasn't been walked since noon."

Ari stuffed the rest of his cupcake into his mouth. He jumped up, his chair scraping the linoleum floor. "Okay."

He scooted around the table and grabbed Buster. He gave the big dog a shove toward the basement stairs. "Be right back," Ari said.

Buster trotted up the stairs. Ari followed close behind. The three of us waited to give them time to leave. Then we huddled together over the table.

"Are you really going to do it, Frankie?" Eduardo whispered. "Are you really going to put that stuff in his drink?"

I nodded. "Yes. Just a few drops of this, and he'll disappear. Then he'll see that magic is real."

I jumped up and crossed the room. I had tossed my jacket over the arm of the couch. I picked it up and dug the plastic bottle from the pocket.

I carried the bottle to the table. I raised it in front of me. The three of us gazed at the bright yellow liquid at the bottom of the bottle.

"Here goes," I murmured. I took a deep breath. Then I unscrewed the cap. I held the bottle over Ari's glass—and poured the secret formula into his lemonade.

SLAPPY HERE, EVERYONE.

Haha. Frankie is playing a good joke on Ari. The only problem is, he won't be able to see the sick look on Ari's face when he realizes what Frankie has done to him!

I'm a good magician, too.

I'm so good, I have you in my control. Now watch what I can do. When I say *Abracadabra*, I can make you turn the page. Watch . . .

Abracadabra!

Melody had her eyes on Ari's lemonade glass. She grinned and rubbed her hands together. "This is so totally evil."

Eduardo stared at the empty bottle in my hand and didn't say anything.

I heard Ari's footsteps upstairs. He called out something to his mother.

I jumped up and darted across the room. I jammed the plastic bottle into my coat pocket.

I started to toss the jacket back onto the couch. But my magic wand fell out of the other pocket. It hit the floor and rolled across the linoleum.

I was picking it up when Ari came back down the stairs, followed by Buster. "What are you doing with the wand?" Ari demanded. "Are you sure you're ready for a pointy stick? You might poke your eye out." He laughed at his own bad joke.

"Not funny," I said. "*You're* the one who isn't ready. We're getting you a training wand!"

Melody and Eduardo laughed. Ari just scowled.

I sat down and placed the wand beside my cupcake plate. Buster licked my hand some more. I didn't try to push him away. I was too busy concentrating on Ari's lemonade glass.

Go ahead. Drink it. Drink it . . .

Ari reached for his glass.

I sucked in a deep breath and held it.

Before Ari could drink, Buster jumped up. The big dog snapped his teeth open and grabbed my magic wand off the table.

"Hey—stop!" I cried. I swiped at it. Missed.

Buster took off, running across the rec room. I hurtled after him. "Stop him. He'll chew it to bits."

Melody and Eduardo came darting after me. I dove at him. Tried to wrap my arms around his neck. But he dodged to the side, and I stumbled into the couch.

The dog stared at me, the wand locked tightly between his teeth. I knew he was playing with me. But I was in no mood to play. Besides, the wand had cost thirty-five dollars!

Buster scampered along the far wall. Melody and Eduardo had him cornered. Eduardo grabbed the end of the wand.

"Careful!" I cried. "Don't pull it too hard. It'll break."

Buster gave up the game. He opened his jaws and let the wand slide out. Eduardo pulled it carefully away from him and handed it to me.

"Yuck!" I cried. "It's covered in dog slobber."

Ari laughed. He hadn't moved from the table. "Buster wants to be a magician, too. He could probably teach you some tricks, Frankie."

Grumbling to myself, I wiped the wand off on the leg of my jeans. The three of us took our places at the table.

"This is an awesome meeting," Ari said. "We should name Buster president of the club!" He laughed.

I gazed at Ari's lemonade glass. It was time to get this going. The dog was trying to ruin my big plan.

I raised my glass high. "Cheers, everyone!" I said.

The others raised their glasses. "Cheers!"

We all drank. The lemonade was cold and sweet.

Ari drank his glass all the way down without taking a breath.

No one spoke. I clasped my hands tightly together in my lap. Melody, Eduardo, and I didn't move. We watched Ari. And waited . . . waited for the formula to do its thing.

11

I realized I was holding my breath. I let it out slowly, keeping my eyes on Ari.

He smiled at me and twirled his empty lemonade glass between his hands.

Ari—disappear! I thought. *Why aren't you disappearing?*

Mystical Marvin vanished in a flash.

Ari's smile stayed frozen on his face. He tapped his glass on the tabletop. His eyes were locked on mine.

"I overheard your plan," he said finally.

I squinted at him. "Excuse me?"

"I didn't take Buster outside. I waited upstairs and listened to you. I heard you were going to put something in my lemonade. Something to make me disappear."

My breath caught in my throat. "But—"

"So, guess what, Frankie?" Ari said. "When you chased after Buster and your magic wand, I switched glasses with you."

"No!" I cried. "No way!"

Melody and Eduardo turned to me. Their eyes grew wide.

"Frankie? Where *are* you?" Melody cried.

Eduardo pointed at me with a trembling finger. "You—you—" he sputtered.

"Huh?" I glanced down. *Where are my hands? Where are my legs? Where is my BODY?*

I knew what had happened, but I didn't want to believe it.

I jumped to my feet, knocking the chair over. It clattered noisily to the floor, but my heart was clattering even louder!

"I-I'm invisible!" I cried.

Melody and Eduardo stared openmouthed. They were too shocked and horrified to say anything.

"Can you hear me?" I demanded in a trembling voice. "I know you can't see me. But can you *hear* me?"

Melody and Eduardo nodded. "We can hear you," Melody said in a whisper. "But . . . you're invisible, Frankie. You're completely invisible."

Ari was still smiling. "Whoa, Frankie! I guess you were right," he said. "I guess Mystical Marvin's magic *is* real after all!" He laughed. "You win!"

My brain was spinning. I crept up behind Ari and mussed up his hair with both hands.

"Watch it!" he cried out, and tried to swat

me away. But he didn't even come close.

"Wow!" I cried. The truth was finally dawning on me. "I really am invisible. This is totally awesome! I can do anything I want!"

I grabbed Ari's chair. I tilted it all the way back and sent it crashing to the floor. He screamed and hit the floor hard. "Stop it, you idiot!" he shouted.

"Come and get me!" I said.

How awesome is this?

I sneaked up behind Eduardo and tickled him till he begged me to stop. I hoisted Buster off the floor and dropped him in Melody's lap.

The dog whimpered and gazed all around. Even *he* realized something was seriously weird.

Ari pulled himself off the floor and stood his chair back on its legs. I darted to the table, raised the glass pitcher high, and poured the lemonade onto Ari's head.

The lemonade oozed over his hair, down his forehead, and onto his shirt. Spluttering, he spun around, swinging his fists. But he couldn't see me. He didn't come close.

I tossed back my invisible head and laughed. "Anything! I can do *anything*! This is so *awesome*!"

I picked Ari's backpack up from beside the couch. I opened it and dumped everything out on the floor.

Ari screamed angrily and began calling me every name he could think of. I took his baseball cap and jammed it down over his sticky wet head.

"Aren't you sorry you traded glasses with me?" I cried.

Melody jumped to her feet and came walking toward me. "Whoa. Hold on a minute, Frankie," she said. She was looking the wrong way. I'd already moved to the stairs.

"What could be more fun than being invisible?" I said. "I'm so glad it wasn't wasted on Ari."

"But just stop for a second," Melody said. "How long have you been invisible? At least ten minutes, right?"

"I . . . guess," I replied.

"Well, shouldn't you be coming back now?" Melody said. "Do you feel yourself coming back to normal?"

I thought about it. "No. Not really," I answered finally.

"So aren't you just a tiny bit worried?" Melody said. "I mean . . . what if you *never* come back?"

12

I slumped into one of the big green armchairs across from the couch. "You sure know how to ruin a party," I said.

Melody sighed. "Just saying."

"The formula will wear off in a few more minutes," I said. "Remember? Mystical Marvin returned to normal pretty soon after we went backstage."

Ari wiped his sticky, wet hair with a cloth napkin from the table. "You never looked better, Frankie. Really."

He started to say more, but we heard footsteps on the basement stairs. Ari's mother poked her head into the rec room. "I came down for the lemonade pitcher and—"

She stopped. Her mouth dropped open. She stared at Ari's sticky, wet hair. "What *happened* to you? You spilled the lemonade?"

"Not exactly," Ari muttered.

"We . . . uh . . . tried a new magic trick," Melody said.

"Yeah. And it didn't work," Eduardo chimed in.

Mrs. Goodwyn rubbed her forehead. "That must have been quite a trick. Where's Frankie? Did he leave?"

"Yeah. He disappeared," Ari said. He glanced at Eduardo and Melody, signaling for them not to say anything.

"I didn't see him leave," Mrs. Goodwyn said.

"Yeah. He just vanished," Ari told her. "I think he remembered something he had to do."

She placed a hand on Ari's shoulder, then instantly jerked it away. "Yuck. Your T-shirt is soaked."

"It was part of the magic trick," Ari said. "It was supposed to stay dry. But like I said, the trick was a flop."

Mrs. Goodwyn collected the lemonade pitcher and started back up the stairs. "Maybe you guys should stick to card tricks," she said.

"That's what *I* said!" Melody exclaimed.

We didn't talk until we heard her footsteps above us in the kitchen. "Now what?" Melody said. "Frankie, where are you?"

"I'm sitting right next to you," I said. I squeezed her wrist. "Can you feel that?"

She nodded. "Yes. But you're still invisible."

I sighed. "Tell me something I don't know."

"The formula is probably going to wear off any second," Eduardo said. I told you. He is always the optimist, the cheerful one.

"Probably," I said. I jumped to my feet. "Come on. Let's not sit around and be tense. Let's have some fun while I'm still invisible."

"Fun?" Eduardo said. "What do you mean?"

They couldn't see my grin. "Let's go scare some people!" I said.

13

Our bikes lay on their sides, scattered across Ari's front yard. We jumped on them and took off down the street, heading toward school.

We whooped and hollered and made sure people saw us coming. And of course, we got an awesome reaction when people saw my bike—appearing to drive itself!

Horns honked. A blue SUV squealed to a stop and nearly hit a mailbox. People shouted out their car windows.

"How do you do that?"

"Hey—that bike is moving on its own! Somebody stop it!"

"Is that a joke?"

"Is that a motorbike?"

"How do you get that bike to go uphill?"

The four of us laughed and kept rolling.

Some guys from the high school were crossing the street at the playground. They were tossing a soccer ball back and forth. But they stopped when they saw us.

They stepped in front of us, forcing us to stop. "That bike doesn't have a rider," one of them said. He cradled the soccer ball under his arm and squinted at my bike.

"Yes it does," Melody said. "An invisible boy is riding it."

The boys laughed. "You're funny," a tall dude with short, spiked blond hair said sarcastically. Then he added: "Funny-looking." I knew him. His name was Richie. He always acted like a total jerk.

I tugged the soccer ball from his hands. I raised it to the top of his head and made it spin.

"Hey—!" He grabbed for the ball. But he wasn't fast enough. I swung the ball away from him. Then I made it spin on top of his friend's head.

He grabbed for the ball. But I grabbed it first and tossed it toward the basket.

They all stared at it in confusion.

I jumped on my bike and started to pedal. I glanced back and saw their startled looks as my bike appeared to ride off by itself.

I heard Richie's words as I rolled away. "Tell the invisible boy if he comes back, I'll give him an invisible nosebleed."

Tough dude.

Six or seven middle grade kids were playing basketball on the court near the teachers' parking lot. I pedaled up beside the court and rested my bike against the chain-link fence.

My three friends caught up with me. They jumped off their bikes and set them down in the grass.

"That was a riot!" Eduardo exclaimed. "That dude Richie didn't know what hit him!"

For some reason, that made all four of us laugh. Some of the basketball players looked up at the sound of our laughter.

I recognized two of the players—Billy Shenkman and DeShawn Jackson. "Let's mess these guys up," I said.

I trotted onto the court. DeShawn was putting on a dribbling show, running circles around the other players. Of course, he didn't see me.

I grabbed the ball easily from his hands. Then I began dribbling toward the basket.

I moved slowly and bounced the ball high so everyone could see clearly that the ball was dribbling on its own. I glanced around. The players had all stopped moving. Their eyes were following the ball, and wide with disbelief.

I took a jump shot from the foul line. The ball clanged against the side of the hoop but didn't go in.

DeShawn and Billy were shaking their heads. They charged over to grab the rebound. But I took the ball and dribbled away.

"Am I dreaming this?" DeShawn cried.

My three friends watched from the other side of

the fence. They were laughing and slapping high fives. The basketball players just stood with their mouths open, shaking their heads and muttering.

I took another shot. Missed again.

I never was any good at basketball.

I grabbed the rebound and stood dribbling in place.

"I have to go home," Billy told his friends. "This is seriously freaking me out!"

"I keep thinking maybe it's just the wind," another guy said.

"It's not the wind," DeShawn told him. "Definitely not the wind."

I raised the ball and tossed it to DeShawn.

"Who threw that?" DeShawn demanded, raising his eyes to the other players.

"No one!" one of them exclaimed. "No one threw it, DeShawn!"

DeShawn saw my three friends watching from the other side. "Hey—!" he called to them. "Did you see what just happened here?"

"See *what*?" Ari shouted back.

"I didn't see anything," Melody said. "Why'd you stop your game?"

DeShawn didn't reply.

Shaking his head, Billy turned and started to stride quickly off the court. "Catch you guys later," he called back to his friends. "I'm out of here."

"Do you believe in ghosts?" one of the players said.

"I don't know *what* I believe in," his friend answered. Then they scattered and hurried away from the playground.

"That was awesome!" Eduardo said. "I think you totally messed with their minds, Frankie!"

We enjoyed a good laugh.

I saw Lucy and Deirdre, two girls from our class, across the playground grass. They were tossing a Frisbee back and forth.

"Catch this," I told my friends. "This will be classic."

I ran between them. I waited for Lucy to toss the Frisbee. Then I dove in front of Deirdre and grabbed the Frisbee in midair.

She gasped in surprise as I took off running. I ran past her and then just kept running, holding the Frisbee over my head.

I knew it looked to them as if the Frisbee were sailing for *miles*.

Both girls shouted in amazement. I kept running full speed until I was off the playground. I crossed the street and kept going. I knew they'd be talking about the day the Frisbee took off *forever*.

But I wasn't finished. I stopped for a few seconds to catch my breath. Then, holding the Frisbee high, I crossed the street and came charging back at them.

They cried out in amazement as they watched the Frisbee sail toward them. I shoved it into Deirdre's hands and kept running. I glanced back to see them both staring at each other. Deirdre held the Frisbee carefully, as if it were alive! They didn't know what to say.

I joined my friends at the sidewalk. Everyone agreed I had pulled off a great stunt. "I'm having an awesome time!" I exclaimed. "Have I ever had so much fun? I don't think so."

Melody's expression turned serious. "Let's just take a break here, Frankie," she said.

"Why? What's the problem?"

"The problem is, you're still invisible," she said. "Sit down, okay? Just take a breath."

I sat down on the grass. "Okay. You can't see me, but I'm sitting. Now what?"

Eduardo pulled out his phone. "It's been nearly an hour," he told Melody.

"Yeah. It's almost dinnertime," Ari said. "I've got to get home."

Melody ignored him. "Frankie, where are you? I'm not exactly sure where you are."

"I'm right in front of you," I said.

"Well, maybe you have to concentrate," she said. "Sit still and concentrate. Concentrate on coming back."

I let out a long breath. "Okay. I'm concentrating."

The four of us were silent for a long moment.

"Concentrating," I murmured. I had my eyes shut tight. I really *was* focused hard on coming back. "Concentrate."

Eduardo bent down until his face was right

over mine. "Do you feel any different, Frankie? Do you feel like you're starting to change?"

I didn't answer right away. I was concentrating on my body, my skin. I gazed down at where my arms should be. Maybe if I stared hard enough, they would come back into view.

"No," I said finally. "No. I don't feel any different."

Eduardo frowned. I could see the worry in his eyes. "Frankie," he said, "the formula. Do you think maybe you drank too much of it?"

14

"Maybe the formula shouldn't be mixed with lemonade," I muttered.

"Well, don't blame *me*!" Ari exclaimed. "It wasn't *my* idea. *You* put that stuff in the lemonade, Frankie. It isn't my fault."

"I know it isn't your fault," I replied. "I was just saying . . ."

"It's getting late," Melody said. "My parents will start to wonder where I am."

Parents?

I hadn't even thought about my parents.

"I . . . can't let my parents see me like this," I said.

"You mean *not* see you like this!" Ari joked.

Melody slapped him on the arm. "Not funny," she told him.

I suddenly had a heavy feeling of dread in the pit of my stomach. "My parents aren't good in emergencies," I said. "When something bad happens, they just freak out. They start screaming at each other and running around in circles like crazy people."

"You've got to tell them, Frankie," Melody said.

"No, I can't," I said. "I have to wait . . . till the formula wears off. Then I'll tell them all about it."

"Why don't you call them and say you're going to stay over at my house?" Eduardo said.

"But your parents—" I started.

"They're away," he said. "My cousin Natalie is staying with my sister and me. And you're invisible. She won't even know you're there."

"That's perfect," I said. "Thanks, Eduardo. You're a good friend."

"You're *not* a good friend," Ari said. "You tried to make me disappear."

"YOU dropped me onto the stage in front of the whole school. I wish you *would* disappear!" I exclaimed.

"Why don't you try drinking more lemonade?" Ari said.

I stumbled toward Ari and grabbed him around the waist. I guess I kind of lost it. I tackled him to the ground and held him down.

He thrashed at me, trying to throw me off him. "I'm sorry! I'm sorry! Get off me, Frankie!" he screamed.

"Hey—you'd better stop!"

I heard Melody's cry. And turned to see two

teachers from the middle school walking up to us. I recognized them right away. Miss Barlow and Mr. Schein.

Miss Barlow is our teacher. She looks a lot like my grandmother. She's short and very thin, with curly white hair and crinkly blue eyes.

Mr. Schein is the music teacher. Everyone thinks he's cool because he has long black hair, a real bushy mustache, and always looks like he hasn't shaved for two or three days.

Their eyes grew wide as they stared down at Ari.

"Ari, what are you doing?" Mr. Schein asked. "Wrestling with yourself?"

He finally stopped wrestling. I dropped my arms to my sides and tried to catch my breath.

"Uh . . . it's a new workout," Ari said. "My dad takes yoga classes, and he taught me how to do it."

The teachers stared down at him. I'm pretty sure they didn't believe him.

Then Melody spoke up and surprised me by telling the two teachers the truth. "Mr. Schein? Miss Barlow? We need help."

Eduardo grabbed her arm. "Uh . . . Melody . . . wait."

But Melody had decided to tell them what was going on here.

"What's the problem?" Miss Barlow asked. "Does Ari need help? Is that why he's on his back on the grass?"

Ari jumped to his feet. "No. I don't need help," he said.

"Frankie does," Melody said.

Mr. Schein scratched the back of his head. "Frankie? Frankie Miller? Frankie isn't here."

"Yes he is," Melody said. "He's here, but he's invisible."

Both teachers laughed.

"It isn't funny," I said.

Mr. Schein gasped. Miss Barlow glanced around, trying to find me.

"Melody is telling the truth," I said. "I drank a magician's potion, and it turned me invisible."

"See? I'm telling the truth," Melody said. "Can you help us? Do you have any ideas?"

The two teachers exchanged glances.

"Hey, no problem," Mr. Schein said. "Miss Barlow and I know how to handle that."

15

"All you have to do is tickle him," Miss Barlow said. "That works every time, doesn't it, Mr. Schein?"

"Every time," he said.

She reached out both hands and moved her fingers, tickling the air. "Tickle, tickle!" she cried.

Mr. Schein joined in, making tickling motions with both hands.

Then both teachers walked off, laughing.

They stopped at the corner and turned back to us. "Where did Frankie's voice come from?" Mr. Schein shouted. "Oh, I know. From your phone, right?"

"Very clever," Miss Barlow said.

They crossed the street and faded from sight.

"They didn't believe us," Melody said. "Sorry, Frankie."

"Yeah. Sorry, Frankie," Ari said sarcastically. "But I've got to get home." He climbed onto his bike. "Glad you liked my mom's lemonade!" He tossed back his head and hee-hawed like a donkey. Then he furiously pedaled away.

"He *poisoned* me," I said. "And then he just rides away laughing his head off!"

"You tried to poison *him*," Melody replied. "What if your plan had worked? How bad would you feel if you made Ari invisible, and he couldn't come back?"

"Not very," I said.

"I just thought of something," Eduardo said. "Tomorrow is Class Photo Day at school."

"You're kidding me!" I cried. "Tell me that isn't true. I'm going to be invisible in my class photo?"

"Maybe you'll come back before tomorrow," Eduardo said.

"Maybe I won't," I said. "It isn't fair. It just isn't fair. Who wants to be invisible in his class photo?"

They both stared at where they thought I was standing. They didn't know what to say.

I let out a long moan. I couldn't help it. I was getting really upset. Being invisible had been a lot of fun for an hour. A lot of laughs.

But I didn't feel like laughing anymore. It was time to get back to my real life. I moaned again. "What am I going to do?" I cried.

"Go back to Mystical Marvin," Melody said.

"Yeah. She's right," Eduardo chimed in. "He's the only one who can bring you back."

"We should have thought of it sooner," Melody said. "He'll know exactly what to do."

"You can stop being upset," Eduardo said. "He'll get you back in no time."

I hesitated. "But . . . he'll know I stole some of his formula. Maybe he'll be too angry to help me."

"That's dumb," Melody said. "He'll help you even if he *is* angry. He'll feel sorry for you."

"Let's go to the theater," Eduardo said. He pulled my bike up from the grass and waited for me to climb on.

I sat down and curled my hands around the handlebars. "I'm starting to feel better," I said. "You're right. We should have thought of this sooner."

Melody and Eduardo climbed onto their bikes and we began to ride toward the Town Center. It was nearly dinnertime. Cars jammed the streets. Evening rush hour. People driving home after their jobs.

Of course, we got a lot of attention from people in cars. We were riding single file along the curb. My bike was in the middle. People saw the pedals moving up and down—but no one on the bike.

Cars honked and people shouted at us. One car squealed to a stop and four passengers stuck their heads out the windows to gawk at us.

I kept my eyes straight ahead. It would have been a riot to watch, but there was nothing funny about this anymore.

I had only one thing on my mind—getting to the theater and asking Mystical Marvin to reverse the potion and make me visible again.

The Town Center wasn't far from our neighborhood. But to me, the trip seemed to take hours. Finally, we rolled up in front of the theater. I let my bike fall to the sidewalk and hurried up to the entrance doors. Melody and Eduardo were close behind me.

I peered through the glass doors. The box office inside was dark. The whole entry hall was dark.

A large poster stood at the side of the entrance. It showed Mystical Marvin in his billowing red cape. He had a magic wand perched in one hand. His blue eyes appeared to glow above his smile.

I walked over to the poster. A yellow banner had been strung across the front. And on the banner, in big black type, were the words:

PERFORMANCE CANCELED.

Why?

Where was *Mystical Marvin?*

16

I read the two words over and over. Melody and Eduardo stared at the poster beside me. "No show tonight," Eduardo said.

"Let's see what's up," I said.

I moved to the entrance doors and tried pulling them open.

They were locked.

"We can go to the dressing room entrance in back," I said. "Maybe that door is open. If it isn't, we can shout for someone to let us in."

We walked our bikes to the alley at the side of the theater. Several trash cans were lined up along the low stone wall across from the theater. We edged our way past them and followed the alley toward the back.

The sun had gone down, and the alley was dark. Melody's and Eduardo's long shadows moved beside them. I didn't have a shadow. That made me feel sad. And even more frightened.

I stopped in front of a narrow metal door cut

into the side of the theater. "Let's try it," I said.

The door didn't have a handle or a doorknob. I found a narrow opening. I slid my fingers in and pulled the door open. I leaned forward and peered in.

I could see the rows of seats in the theater. We were at one of the side exits. "Let's go," I said.

We stepped into the theater. The auditorium was completely dark. The stage was lit by a single lamp on a pole in the center.

It took a few seconds for my eyes to adjust. "It smells so stale in here," I murmured. My voice sounded muffled in the giant space.

"Maybe they don't ever clean it," Melody whispered.

"It's a very old theater," Eduardo said. "My grandfather says he used to come here when he was a boy."

I turned and gazed at the stage. It was still set up for Mystical Marvin's act. The red curtain was pulled open. The water tank still stood near the wings.

I let out a long sigh of relief. "At least his stuff is still here," I said. "That means he'll be back."

"Anybody here?" Melody called in a loud voice. I jumped. I wasn't expecting her to shout. "Hello? Anybody here?" Her voice rang off the high walls.

Silence.

"No one here," Eduardo whispered. "Maybe we should come back later. I mean—"

"No!" I said. "We have to look backstage. Maybe he's back there." I started to the narrow passageway that led past the stage. "Follow me."

"We *can't* follow you," Melody said. "Did you forget?"

I let Melody lead the way backstage. Dim light washed over the area from one of the dressing rooms. The chest of props we had seen before had been pushed against one wall.

A row of auditorium seats were lined up beside it. A giant red ball sat in one of the seats. A large poster of King Kong was tilted against another wall.

No sign of Mystical Marvin.

"Anyone here?" Melody called again. "Hello?"

I let out a cry as something bumped me. Something scrambled over my shoes. I tripped over it. Caught myself before I fell.

I peered down. A fat mouse was running toward the dressing rooms. It couldn't see me, so it ran right over my foot!

"Frankie, what's your problem?" Eduardo turned to where he thought I was standing.

"You two aren't afraid of mice, are you?" I replied.

"No," they both said.

"Good," I said.

I heard a clattering sound. It came from the open dressing room.

"Hey! Someone there?" I trotted over to it. Melody and Eduardo were close behind me.

"Whoa!" I saw the janitor at Mystical Marvin's dressing table. The same old guy Melody and I had seen after the performance.

He wore his gray work uniform. The shirt was open, revealing a white T-shirt underneath. His long gray hair fell over his forehead as he worked.

He had a roll of paper towels and a can of some kind of spray cleaner. He was wiping down the top of the dressing table.

He stopped and gazed at Melody and Eduardo. His face twisted in surprise. "Can I help you?" he asked in a gravelly, hoarse voice.

"We're here to talk to Mystical Marvin," Melody said.

The man's eyes narrowed suspiciously. "How'd you get in here?"

"The side door was open," Eduardo said.

The janitor climbed to his feet. "You shouldn't be in here. If you are looking for autographs—"

"No. We don't want autographs," Melody said. "We need to see Mystical Marvin. It's . . . it's a real emergency."

The man rubbed his stubbly white whiskers. "I'm the only one here," he said. "I have to ask you to leave. The show is canceled."

"But is he nearby?" Eduardo said. "When is he coming back?"

"I don't know. You're out of luck."

"It's really important," Melody said, her voice rising. "Please. Do you know where he is?"

The man shook his head. "No one does."

"Excuse me?" Eduardo said. "No one knows where he is?"

"He disappeared," the janitor replied.

"You mean he quit the show?" Eduardo asked.

"No. He disappeared." The man picked up his roll of paper towels and the can of cleaner. "I'm telling you the truth. I saw him take a drink from a little glass bottle. And then he disappeared. Flash. Disappeared. I saw it with my own eyes."

"And . . . you don't know where he went?" Melody demanded.

"No. Not a clue. No one knows where he is. He disappeared after Saturday's show—and he never came back."

SLAPPY HERE, EVERYONE.

What did the doctor say when the Invisible Man came to his office?

"Sorry, I can't see you now."

Hahahaha.

Didn't Mystical Marvin ever hear the old saying, *The show must go on*? Maybe he thinks people won't come to a magic show when you can't see who is doing the tricks. Ha.

Is Mystical Marvin finished in show business?

Is Frankie just plain *finished*?

We'll see . . .

Or maybe we *won't* see! Hahahaha.

17

Dinner at Eduardo's house was weird.

Veronica is only six, and she's a terror. She's seriously wild. I mean she screeches like a hyena and laughs all the time and thinks it's really funny to sneak up on you and shove you in the belly as hard as she can.

I was lucky to be invisible. Veronica couldn't shove me or punch me or beat me up.

Their cousin Natalie, who was staying with them, is probably eighteen or nineteen. She is tall with green eyes and and long black hair. She walks in slow motion, her hair swaying like a horse's tail behind her.

She never took her eyes off her phone. Seriously. She never looked up from her phone screen. She held the phone in one hand, texted all through dinner, and didn't say two words to Eduardo or Veronica.

Eduardo was the only one who knew I was sitting at the dinner table with them. I sat next to him, and he kept slipping me food when no one was watching.

Natalie had brought home a big bag of McDonald's, and Eduardo kept handing me chicken nuggets and fries under the table.

"Why didn't you get me a Happy Meal?" Veronica demanded in her loud, whiny voice. "Why didn't I get a toy?"

"You have enough toys," Natalie told her. She just kept typing with one thumb as she ate her Quarter Pounder.

"Those toys are boring, anyway," Eduardo told his sister.

She threw a chicken nugget across the table and it bounced off his forehead. "They are not!"

Natalie went into the kitchen to get more ketchup.

I decided to have a little fun with Veronica. I crept up behind her. I pulled two chicken nuggets from her pack. I raised them high and made them dance in the air in front of her.

She gasped and made a grab for them. I swung them out of her reach. "Eduardo—look!" she cried. "Those nuggets—"

I dropped them back onto the table.

"What's wrong with the nuggets?" Eduardo asked, acting innocent.

"They—they jumped around in the air!" his sister stammered. "Didn't you see them?"

"Chicken nuggets don't fly," Eduardo said.

"But—but—!" Veronica sputtered. She picked one up and examined it closely.

"Stop making up stuff," Eduardo said. "It isn't funny."

She shoved the nuggets away. "Think I'll just eat the fries."

Eduardo's room is small. His wall is covered with baseball posters, and the whole space is cluttered with piles of sports cards and framed photos of Mets players and sports magazines he reads. Two shelves are jammed with the shiny silver trophies he won for basketball and Little League baseball.

Twin beds were squeezed into one end of the room. The beds had New York Mets orange-and-blue quilts over them.

"Take that one," Eduardo said, pointing to the bed next to the window.

"What a crummy day," I moaned. "I am so stressed out, I don't know if I can fall asleep."

"Count invisible sheep!" Eduardo said.

I had to laugh. He almost never makes jokes. I knew he was trying to cheer me up.

"You'll probably be back to normal in the morning," he said.

"You think?"

I wasn't so sure.

I climbed into bed and stretched out on my back. The bed was soft and comfortable. I couldn't stop yawning. Maybe I *could* fall asleep. I tugged the quilt up to my chin and shut my eyes.

Just as I was drifting off, Eduardo's cousin Natalie burst into the room. Light from the hallway washed in through the open door.

"Just wanted to say good night," Natalie said. "I—" She stopped and stared at my bed.

She turned to Eduardo. "Hey, why did you mess up the other bed? I'm not making two beds."

Eduardo raised his head from his pillow. He pretended to be half-asleep. "Uh . . . I didn't do it. The dog did it."

Natalie rolled her eyes. "Yeah, sure. Did you forget? You don't have a dog."

Eduardo thought for a minute. "We don't?"

"No," Natalie said. "You don't. So why did you mess up the other bed?"

"I didn't do it," he told her. "The invisible boy did it."

She sighed. "Weirdo." She spun away, closing the door behind her.

Eduardo turned to me. He shrugged. "I told her the truth."

"Who would believe the truth?" I replied.

During the night, I had a very bold dream. I was onstage in a huge theater, doing a magic act.

I wore Mystical Marvin's red cape. And sometimes in the dream, I had his crinkly blond hair. I was me and I was Mystical Marvin at the same time.

I did the levitating trick, and the crowd went wild.

Then I did a crazy trick you can only do in a dream. I rode a tiger across the stage and then I made the tiger vanish into thin air.

The audience rose to their feet and gave me a standing ovation.

I had the biggest smile on my face. And it was *my face.*

Yes, I had a face in the dream. I had eyes and a nose. And hands and arms. I was *me.* I was back.

Back to normal.

And I took a deep bow as the audience continued to stand and cheer. I wanted to cheer, too. Because I wasn't invisible anymore. I could see myself and so could everyone else.

I woke with the dream still in my head. I blinked. I could still hear the applause.

I sat straight up, wide awake now. I gazed around Eduardo's room, and a smile spread over my face for real.

I'm back.

I'm me.

I'm finally back.

I glanced down at my hands. And I let out a groan. My smile drooped. I shoved the quilt down and looked for my feet.

No.

No. No. No.

I pounded my invisible chest with both invisible fists.

I wasn't back in real life. I was only back in the dream.

I sank onto the pillow. *Maybe I'll NEVER come back!* I thought.

What am I going to do?

18

Natalie had to take Veronica to her kindergarten class early, so Eduardo and I were alone in the kitchen for breakfast.

He poured us big bowls of Frosted Flakes, and we sat across from each other crunching away. "Why are you grinning?" I asked him.

"It looks funny," he said. "Your spoon looks like it's floating by itself in midair, and then the cereal just suddenly disappears somewhere, like into a hole."

"The hole is my mouth," I said. "I don't think it's too funny."

"That formula should have worn off by now," Eduardo said. "I had an idea last night."

I set down my spoon. "An idea?"

"After school," he said. "Let's go to the magic store. You know. Abracadabra 'N' Stuff. The place where we buy all our props and tricks."

"What will we do there?" I asked.

"That guy Jerome knows all about magic,"

Eduardo said. "Maybe he knows about disappearing tricks. Maybe he'll know about an antidote."

"Hmmmmm." I thought about it. It was a long shot. But I was desperate. "Okay," I said. "Good idea, Eduardo. Let's do it."

I raised the glass and took a long drink of orange juice.

Eduardo laughed. "Sorry," he said. "But it just looks so funny."

I didn't feel like going to school. But I didn't want to hang around by myself until it was time to go to Abracadabra 'N' Stuff.

I took my seat in the back row. I left my backpack in my locker. I knew a floating backpack would make everyone upset.

I glimpsed Ari in his seat on the other side of the room. He was slapping knuckles with the kid next to him. Ari had a big grin on his face. Typical.

I saw Melody in the front row. She was reading something on her phone. Eduardo sat two seats down from her. He was just staring straight ahead, waiting for class to begin.

Miss Barlow stepped into the room and perched on the edge of her desk. She was wearing the long skirt and baggy sweater she always wore. She raised her little black notebook and scanned a page.

"Since it's Class Photo Day, I don't want to use

up time taking the roll," she said. "Just speak up if you're not here."

Funny. A few kids laughed.

She glanced around the room. Her eyes stopped at my empty seat. "Frankie Miller? Are you here?"

I didn't answer. If I did, it would make everyone crazy.

"Frankie?" she repeated. "Has anyone seen him?"

"He's here, but he's invisible," Ari shouted.

That got a really big laugh.

It was all a big joke to him.

"It's a beautiful day," Miss Barlow said. "We're going outside now for our class photo. The bleachers have been set up. When you get out there, the photographer will tell you how to line up."

I let out a long sigh. Class Photo Day and I was invisible.

Everyone began streaming out the door. To my surprise, Eduardo appeared in front of me. "Here," he said. "I brought you this."

He held up a blue jacket and a Mets cap.

"What's that for?" I demanded. "It isn't cold outside."

"Put them on," Eduardo said. "At least you'll be in the photo."

"Great. A jacket, a cap, and no face," I muttered.

"But you'll be there," Eduardo said. "And when you come back to normal, you'll think it's funny.

You'll see the jacket and cap and you'll laugh."

"Hope you're right," I said. I pulled on the cap and then the Mets jacket. They both disappeared as soon as I put them on.

"Nice try," I said to Eduardo.

"Sorry," he muttered. He turned and I followed him out the door.

Ready for the worst Class Photo Day of my life.

Frankie, I told myself, *don't forget to smile.*

A bright sun was already high in the sky. Bleachers had been set up on the grass at the side of the school building.

The photographer was a young man in jeans and a red plaid lumberjack jacket. He had a black wool cap pulled down on his head, a stubbly black beard, and a silver ring in one ear. His camera was set up on a tripod facing the bleachers.

"Tall people at the top," he was shouting. "Only short people on the bottom bleacher."

"What about invisible people?" I shouted.

No one seemed to hear me. They were all eager to get into their places on the bleachers.

I followed Eduardo. I knew he was heading to the top row.

Why am I doing this? I asked myself. I didn't have an answer. My feelings were so mixed up.

"First row, everyone sit down," the photographer was shouting. "Fill in the second row.

Everyone squeeze in. Come on, people. Squeeze in tighter. Don't be shy."

I edged onto the top row and raised my eyes. "Hey—!"

Somehow, I'd lost Eduardo. I turned and saw him standing on the far end of the second row.

Someone bumped against me. At first, I saw a bright purple polo shirt. Then I raised my eyes and realized I was standing next to Ari. Of course, he didn't see me.

He edged sideways and bumped me again.

"Watch where you're going," I snapped.

His eyes bulged in surprise. "You're here?"

"Yes, I am," I said. "I don't want to miss Class Photo Day."

He snickered. "This will be the best photo you ever took!"

"How funny are you?" I said. "Not."

I decided to have some fun. We were all squeezed tight on the top bleacher. I bent my knees and jumped. I landed hard and the whole bench shook.

"Hey! Who did that?" a girl cried.

I saw the guy at the end of the bench almost fall off. He stumbled to the side, bumping the kid next to him.

I jumped again. The bench bobbed down, then up.

Kids screamed in surprise. Their hands flew

up as they struggled to keep their balance.

I jumped up and down. "Earthquake!" I shouted.

Arms flailing, kids tumbled off the sides of the top bench. Screams all around. Ari fell into the kids in front of him. They all hit the grass in a pile of arms and legs.

The Invisible Boy Strikes Again! I thought.

Kids were groaning and uttering confused cries. They scrambled to their feet. They shook their heads as they wiped grass stains off their clothes.

Miss Barlow came trotting over. "Is everyone okay? What happened?" she cried in a panic.

"Ari knocked us over," Marla Stolz said. She kept rubbing her shoulder and groaning.

"I didn't do it!" Ari cried. "It was Frankie!"

Miss Barlow squinted at him. "Frankie Miller?"

"Frankie jumped up and down and made us all fall off," Ari said.

"Ari, Frankie Miller isn't here today," the teacher said. "He's absent."

"Can we get everyone back in place?" the photographer shouted. "I have the next class waiting for me."

Kids started to climb back on the bleachers. Ari stayed to argue with Miss Barlow.

"Frankie isn't absent," he told her. "He's here. Only he's invisible."

Miss Barlow laughed. "That's a good one, Ari.

94

Why don't you make yourself invisible and go back up to the top row?"

"It's not a joke!" Ari cried.

"Yes, it is," I whispered in Ari's ear. "It's a hilarious joke." I laughed. "The invisible boy strikes again!"

20

After school, Eduardo and I rode our bikes to Abracadabra 'N' Stuff.

Only something had changed.

The store stood on the corner in a low red-brick building. The sign above the glass door used to have a magician's top hat and a magic wand beside the words *Abracadabra 'N' Stuff*.

But as I leaned my bike against a lamppost, I saw that a new sign had been put up. A painting of a steaming soup bowl stood beside the words *Broth & More Broth*.

"Uh-oh," I muttered. A feeling of dread tightened my stomach. I knew instantly that I was in trouble.

I followed Eduardo into the narrow store. Everything had been changed. A glass counter stood along the wall. Behind the glass, I saw a row of large cooking pots. They appeared to contain soup or something.

I glanced all around. No sign of magic tricks or equipment.

From behind the counter, Jerome greeted Eduardo. He was an older guy with short white hair and a slim face, covered in white stubble. He had lively blue eyes that look like they belong on a much younger guy.

Jerome usually wore a magician's top hat. But today it was replaced with a white chef's cap. And he wore a long white apron over his clothes.

"How do you like the new store?" he asked Eduardo.

Eduardo's mouth hung open. He couldn't hide how surprised he was. "Wh-where is the magic stuff?" he stammered.

"Try some bone broth," Jerome said. He picked up a metal ladle. "I have four flavors. It's all hot. The chicken broth is probably what you'll go for."

"But the magic—"

"That stuff is in the basement, ready to ship out," Jerome said. He scratched his stubbly face. "It didn't sell. How many people are interested in performing magic today? They'd rather stare at their phones."

"You still have your magic stuff?" Eduardo asked.

"Bone broth is the new frozen yogurt," Jerome said. "You'd be surprised. People come in and take two or three quarts home. I'm lucky to get in on the broth thing nice and early."

"My friend needs help—" Eduardo started.

"You and your friends were my best customers,"

Jerome interrupted. "Here. Try a sample of the beef bone broth. No charge. It's all organic. You'll like it."

He ladled the brown broth into a bowl and handed it across the counter to Eduardo. I turned and crept away. I found the stairs at the back of the store and silently made my way down to the basement.

Tall stacks of cartons stood against the wall. This was the magic equipment, ready to be shipped away.

I opened the nearest carton and peered inside. It was packed with folded-up top hats and a bunch of plush rabbits to pull out of the hats.

I didn't know what I was looking for, but there had to be something here that would help me.

I found it in the third carton.

It was a makeup kit, a case containing a long row of tubes of stage makeup. I pulled out the first tube. It was bright white, like clown makeup.

If I smear it over my face, will people be able to see me?

My hand trembled as I carried the tube over to a long mirror that stood on the floor, tilted against the back wall.

I removed the little cap from the tube. Then I squeezed the tube and poured a blob of the white makeup onto my hand. I stared at the little puddle of white—and watched it vanish instantly.

Like Eduardo's Mets cap and jacket.

I couldn't hold back my disappointment, my total frustration. I let out a hoarse cry and tossed the makeup tube to the floor. My heart was pounding.

I ran up the stairs. I ran past Eduardo, who was leaning against the counter, spooning up a dark broth while a smiling Jerome looked on.

I grabbed my bike, dropped onto the seat, and began to pedal. I roared furiously down the street, ignoring the stares and startled cries from people who thought they saw a runaway bike.

I had decided to go home.

But if I had known what was going to happen to me once I got there, I would have stayed far away.

21

I knew the house would be empty. Mom and Dad would still be at work. Maybe I could hang out by myself in my room for a few hours and figure out what to do next.

No way I wanted my parents to know what had happened. As I said before, they are both terrible in emergencies, and they wouldn't be any help at all.

For example: Once, when our old dog started to limp, Dad went into a panic and thought he had to call an ambulance for the dog.

Yes. An ambulance.

That's how crazy my parents get in any kind of crisis.

It turned out the dog had a broken toenail.

That's just one example. And it shows why I didn't want them to know that I was now invisible.

I stopped at the curb when I saw the car was in the driveway. Did that mean they were home?

I crept in through the screen door entrance on

the side of the house. I stopped in the back room we use as a pantry and listened.

I heard their voices in the kitchen.

Why had they stayed home from work? Did they know I wasn't in school? Were they worried about where I was?

I tiptoed across the living room, holding my breath. My room was at the end of the back hall.

I can hide in my room, I decided. *If I'm quiet, they won't know I'm there.*

I wanted to change my clothes. Even though I was invisible, I knew that people could *smell* me! No way to take a shower. But at least I could put on a clean T-shirt.

And, of course, I wanted to think about my next move. I still hoped I'd change back without doing anything. Just a POP, a flash of light, and there I'd be. My old self, with a shadow and a reflection and everything.

But if that didn't happen, what were my choices?

I had to think.

Tiptoeing silently, I was nearly across the living room, stepping into the back hall—when I sneezed.

"Frankie? Is that you?" Dad came running into the living room.

"Frankie? Where are you?"

22

I stopped with a groan. "Hi, Dad."

"Where are you? I can't see you."

"I'm here, Dad," I said in a tiny voice. "I-I'm messed up. I'm invisible."

Mom came running into the room. "I heard Frankie. Where is he?"

"I'm here, Mom,"

"Frankie? Is this a trick?" Dad cried.

"I . . . can explain," I stammered.

"It's a trick?" Dad repeated. "It's a trick, right? Tell me. Is it a trick?" His eyes spun frantically in his head.

"I must be dreaming this," Mom said, pounding her sides with her fists. "Are we living in a horror movie? Is our son really invisible? It's a nightmare. Our son has made himself invisible? No. No. No."

I told you. They are not good in emergencies.

"Let's sit down," I said. "I . . . I know this looks bad. But let me explain."

"Sit down?" Mom cried. "How can you sit down? You're invisible!"

"Who did this to you?" Dad demanded. "Who did this? Should I call the police?"

"Dad, please—" I begged.

I finally got them to sit down at the kitchen table. I pulled a juice box from the fridge and dropped down in a chair across from them. They stared in amazement as the juice box seemed to float in the air.

Dad was drumming his fingers on the tabletop. I asked him three times to stop. But I don't think he could.

Mom had gone very pale. She stared at the floating juice box. She kept wiping tears off her cheeks.

"I did a stupid thing." That's how I started my explanation. "You see, after Mystical Marvin's magic show . . ."

"Should I call nine-one-one?" Dad interrupted. "Do we need the police? Tell me, Frankie."

"What are the police going to do?" Mom asked Dad. "Arrest him for disappearing?"

"Please," I said. "Please don't interrupt me. Okay? Let me tell my story."

I reached across the table. I grabbed Dad's hands to stop them from drumming. I held on to them as I told my story.

Somehow I managed to get the whole story out. How I sneaked out a few teaspoons of Mystical

Marvin's disappearing formula. How I planned to slip them into Ari's lemonade. How my plan was to make him disappear *for only a few minutes.*

They kept shaking their heads and tsk-tsking. But I forced them to be quiet and let me finish.

I told them how Ari switched lemonade glasses, and I became invisible. "It was supposed to wear off, but it didn't," I said. "I spent the night at Eduardo's house, waiting for it to wear off. But . . . here I am, still invisible."

They both squinted at me in silence. Finally, Mom said, "Did you miss Class Photo Day?"

"Donna!" Dad shouted at her angrily. "What's *wrong* with you? What do you care about Class Photo Day?"

Mom shrank back in her chair. "Just asking," she muttered.

Dad jumped to his feet. "We have to take you back to that magician. Marvelous Marv, or whatever his name is."

"It's Mystical Marvin," I said.

"He'll know how to bring you back to normal," Dad said. "Come on. Let's go to the theater."

I set the empty juice box down on the tabletop. "I already did that," I said. "I went to see him. But he wasn't there. He disappeared, too. Vanished. They had to cancel his show."

"Whoooooa." Dad let out a long breath. He shut his eyes. "Let's think. Let's think."

Mom shook her head. She wiped more tears

off her pale cheeks. "Listen to me," she said. "We have only one choice."

"Huh? One choice? I said. "What's that, Mom?"

"Uncle Siggy," she replied.

"Oh no!" I shrieked. "Oh no! Please, Mom—*not* Uncle Siggy!"

23

We drove to the tall building. A sign near the entrance read: UNIVERSITY SCIENCE LAB. Just pulling into the parking lot sent chills down my back.

"I seriously don't want to do this," I said as we climbed the stairs to the double glass doors.

"Listen to me, Frankie," Mom said. "If anyone will know how to reverse that formula, it's your uncle Siggy."

"He's a brilliant scientist," Dad added.

"But he's totally weird!" I exclaimed. "He spent five years studying why slugs are slimy."

"Yes, he's one of the world experts on slugs," Mom said. "But he's not weird. He's eccentric."

"He's a brilliant scientist," Dad repeated. When he gets nervous, he repeats himself a lot.

I hesitated at the entrance. "You really think Siggy can bring me back to normal?"

"He's a brilliant scientist," Dad said.

"He's known all over the world as a chemical genius," Mom said.

"He's brilliant," Dad added.

Siggy is Mom's brother, and no one is ever allowed to say a bad word about him.

He was waiting for us in his lab on the third floor. When he saw Mom and Dad step off the elevator, he tucked his phone into the pocket of his white lab coat.

Siggy is tall and a little bent-over. His head kind of leans toward you all the time. He's bald except for a fringe of brown hair. His round eyeglasses are enormous and make his eyes appear to be bulging out of his head.

He looks a little like my mom, if she were tall and bald and wore glasses and was stooped over. Ha. That's a joke. They don't look like brother and sister in any way.

Mom and Dad had called him. Warned him about my problem. He gazed through his big glasses for a long moment, trying to figure out where I was. Then he hugged Mom and shook hands with Dad. "Frankie isn't looking his best," Siggy said.

That was his idea of a joke. He doesn't really have a sense of humor. I don't think I've ever seen him laugh.

"Frankie, did you ever see the original *Invisible Man* movie starring Claude Rains?"

Siggy asked. "It was made in 1933, in black and white."

I forgot to mention that Siggy is a movie freak. He loves old movies, like the one he just mentioned.

"No," I muttered. "I never saw it."

"This isn't a movie," Dad chimed in. "It's real."

"You should watch it sometime," Siggy said. He pushed his glasses up on his nose. "Well, let's see about solving this problem."

He took out his phone, raised it in front of me, and snapped a few photos of me. Then he studied the photos. "Yep," he said. "You're not there. That's so interesting."

"Can you fix him?" Mom demanded in a trembling voice. "Siggy, can you do anything?"

He patted her shoulder. "I'll do my best, Donna." He motioned to me. "Come back to the lab, Frankie. I want to do a bunch of tests while you tell me how this happened."

So . . . I had to tell the whole sad story all over again. And while I talked, Siggy had his assistants put me through an X-ray machine. Then some other kind of scanner that took photos of my invisible insides.

Then Siggy's assistant took several vials of my blood. This wasn't easy, since my arm was invisible. The blood seemed to be flowing into the glass vials from nowhere. Just from the air!

"Tell me again," Siggy said, rubbing his bald

head. "This magician. Did he tell you anything at all about the formula? Did he give you any hint of what is in it?"

I thought hard. I pictured Mystical Marvin holding the bottle with the yellow formula inside it. I tried to remember . . .

"Yes!" I said finally. "I think he mentioned something about animal saliva."

Siggy's eyes went even wider than usual. "Animal saliva? Really?"

I nodded. "That's what he said."

"Okay, Frankie." Siggy tried to pat me on the back, but he missed. "Let me study the tests. Go back out and wait with your parents. I'll come out as soon as I have an idea."

I slumped back out to the waiting room.

Mom jumped up. She had her hands clasped tensely in front of her. "So? What did Siggy say?"

Dad looked up from his phone. "Can he bring you back?"

"He took a lot of tests," I said. "He's studying them. He said he'd come out when he has an idea."

"So he didn't say he could do it?" Mom's voice was as shrill as a whistle.

"He's looking at the tests," I said. "We have to wait."

So we waited. Mostly in silence. Mom paced back and forth, her hands wrapped in front of her. Dad pretended to read on his phone. But I could tell he wasn't concentrating on anything.

I shut my eyes and tried to make my mind a blank. I didn't want to think about my problem. I didn't want to think about anything.

I must have dozed off. Because when I opened my eyes, Uncle Siggy was standing in front of us, gazing at a clipboard in his hand.

Mom and Dad huddled in front of him. Dad put his arm around Mom's shoulders. "So?" Mom murmured. "So, Siggy?"

"I think I know how to bring Frankie back," Siggy said.

My parents both let out long sighs.

"I studied the tests," Siggy said. "I think I can break down the invisibility molecules."

"How?" I asked. "Break down the molecules? Using what?"

"Acid," Siggy said.

24

"No way!" I cried. "I'm outta here. You're not going to burn me with acid!"

Siggy made a gasping sound and raised his hand to his heart. "Burn you? I'm not going to burn you, Frankie. Don't you trust me?"

I didn't answer. I started to back away, my eyes on the elevator doors.

"You have to listen to your uncle," Dad said. "He's a brilliant man."

"Siggy would never hurt you," Mom said.

I let out a long sigh. I decided to give in. I mean, Siggy was a genius chemical scientist. And I had nowhere else to turn.

He led me to a wooden chair that had a tabletop jutting out from the side. Like an old-fashioned school desk. "Sit down, Frankie," he said softly.

I slid into the chair.

"Are you sitting?" he asked.

"Yes," I said. And to my surprise Siggy leaned down, grabbed a leather belt attached to the chair, and strapped it tightly around my waist.

"I can't see you," he said. "Is that comfortable?"

"If you're not going to hurt me," I replied, "why are you strapping me in?"

"Just so I can find you," he said. "I'll be back. I'm going to go mix the acids now. Stay calm. I haven't lost any patients all day."

His idea of a joke.

"You don't *have* any patients!" I shouted after him. "You're a scientist, remember?" He disappeared back into the lab.

As soon as he was gone, Mom and Dad walked over to the chair. "He knows what he's doing," Dad said.

"Siggy can make an acid that doesn't burn," Mom said. "And just think, Frankie. In a few minutes, we'll all be able to see you again."

I started to say, "What if it doesn't work?"

But my parents were so excited. They looked happy, so I decided not to say anything.

The next ten minutes were tense. Mom and Dad stood awkwardly, staring at each other, unable to think of anything more to say. I sat staring at the lab door, waiting for Siggy to return.

Wild thoughts raced through my head as I waited. I found myself thinking about how I would pay Ari back for doing this to me.

I shut my eyes and tried to stop thinking about him. When I opened them, Siggy came through the lab door. He had a smile on his face, as if he had already succeeded.

He carried a large glass beaker in both hands. The beaker was half filled with a clear liquid. The acid.

"I know you like to perform magic, Frankie," Siggy said, setting the beaker down on a window ledge. "Well, I'm going to perform some magic of my own."

"H-hope you're right," I stammered.

Mom and Dad huddled behind Siggy.

"Since you're nervous about this," Siggy said, "we'll start with something small. Put your hand on the desktop here."

I slid my invisible hand onto the desktop.

"Okay. Hold it very steady," Siggy said. "Spread the fingers out and don't move a muscle, okay?"

"Okay," I said.

"This should have your hand back in seconds," Siggy said. "Just say *Abracadabra*."

He lifted the beaker and held it over the desktop.

"Abracadabra!" I shouted.

Siggy tilted the beaker and poured the liquid over my hand.

25

"YEOOOWWWWWWWWWWW!"

I opened my mouth in a scream that could be heard for miles.

My hand burned as if it were covered in flames. The pain shot up my arm and down my whole body.

"IT BURNS! IT BURRRRRNS!" I wailed.

Siggy took a step back. He set the beaker down. His eyes were lowered to the desk.

Did it work?

Can I see my hand?

No. Still invisible. And the pain roared over me. I waved the hand in the air, trying to cool it down, trying to stop the painful burning.

Siggy pulled a tube from his lab coat pocket. "Frankie, put your hand down on the desk so I can find it. This lotion will stop the stinging in a few minutes."

Stinging?

It didn't feel like stinging. It felt like someone holding a burning torch to my hand.

Siggy rubbed the lotion onto the back of my hand. Then he picked up the beaker and started back to the lab.

"I have to re-mix this," he said. "I'll get it right this time, Frankie. As fast as you can say Abracadabra. No worries."

I waved the hand in the air. The lotion was slowly starting to take away the pain.

Mom and Dad both gazed at the desk in front of the chair.

"No sign of his hand," Dad said. "Maybe Siggy isn't the right person for this."

"Of course he is," Mom argued. "Siggy is a brilliant scientist. I know my brother. He'll keep trying till he gets it right."

"Keep trying?" I cried.

"He was always like that, even when he was a little boy," Mom said. "He wouldn't quit until he mastered something. When he got his first chemistry set, you couldn't get him away from it. You couldn't even get him to eat. He just stayed in his room mixing chemicals for hours."

"Frankie, how is your hand?" Dad asked.

"I think Siggy burned it off," I said. "I can't even feel it now."

Dad turned to Mom. "Donna, we have to go. This was a mistake."

Mom jutted out her chin. "We're not going anywhere. We're not walking out on my brother. Siggy will fix Frankie. I don't have a single doubt."

"Well, I have plenty," Dad said.

While they argued, I silently unfastened the strap that held me down. Then I carefully climbed out of the chair.

Mom and Dad were really going at it. They were chin to chin, arguing about whether to stay or not. Dad kept saying, "Maybe Siggy isn't as brilliant as we thought he was."

That made Mom even angrier. "We're not moving an inch from here!" she shouted.

I crept past them and made my way to the elevator. I knew they wouldn't even notice that I was gone.

I pressed the elevator button. I heard it hum as the elevator car came up. The doors opened. I stepped inside. The doors closed, and I was gone.

I knew exactly where I was going.

26

I slipped into the side door of the theater and glanced around the rows of empty seats in the dimly lit auditorium. The stage was set for Mystical Marvin's show. But the sign outside still read: PERFORMANCE CANCELED.

I made my way backstage. I wasn't surprised that nothing had changed from my last visit. I looked for the old janitor, but he wasn't there today. Mystical Marvin's red robe lay folded on top of the chest of props.

The dressing rooms were all dark. I had hoped that maybe Mystical Marvin had reappeared. Maybe I would find him. And maybe he would tell me how to appear again.

But I didn't really expect to see him. My real reason for going backstage again was different this time.

I wanted to search Mystical Marvin's dressing room. I wanted to go through his things and see if anything—anything at all—might help me return to normal.

The air back here felt stuffy and stale. I saw a tiny lump of gray fur scramble across the floor against the back wall. A mouse.

"Hey—Mystical Marvin!" I shouted his name. Just to make a sound. Just to hear my voice. It was the only way I knew I was real. "Mystical Marvin—*answer* me!"

Silence. Just the echo of my voice against the high walls.

My invisible shoes scraped the concrete floor loudly as I crept to Mystical Marvin's dressing room. I stopped at the open doorway and peered inside.

No one there, of course.

I clicked on the light and stepped in. The dressing table beneath the mirror was filled with small bottles and jars. I dropped onto Mystical Marvin's stool and began to examine them.

What was I looking for? I don't know.

Anything. Anything that might be an antidote. *Anything* that might make me visible again.

My heart began to race and I felt more and more frantic ... more and more desperate ... with each bottle and jar I studied. I went through them all. Sniffed them. Read the labels. Dabbed my finger into the creams and lotions.

No. Nothing helpful on the dressing table. It was mostly makeup and makeup remover. I already knew that makeup wouldn't help me. I also saw many jars of vitamins. He seemed to take a lot of vitamins.

But no antidote.

I jumped up from the stool and darted over to the tall wall cabinet. I flung the door open and raised my eyes to the top shelf.

And there it was.

The small bottle. The bottle of yellow liquid. The formula.

With a groan, I reached up and pulled it down, grasping it carefully in my hand. Breathing hard, I raised the bottle in front of me and gazed at the liquid.

This was the formula that made Mystical Marvin and me disappear. Disappear and not return.

Oh, wait. I spotted another glass bottle beside it. It held a yellow liquid.

Squinting at the label on the front, I read the words: *Appearing Formula.*

"Yessss!" I cried out loud. "Yesss!"

I'd found it. The appearing formula. The antidote.

I grabbed it with a trembling hand. I nearly spilled it as I raised the bottle to my lips.

Yesss! Yesss!

I took a long drink of it.

I was breathing hard as I lowered the bottle. And took another look at the label.

"Oh, no."

I squinted hard at the small, square label. The letters *DIS* had been nearly rubbed out.

It wasn't Appearing liquid after all. It was more Disappearing liquid.

And I had taken a long drink of it.

27

I could still taste it, warm on my tongue. My throat burned.

The warmth of the liquid gave way to cold, and suddenly I began to shiver. My invisible skin felt cold all over. I hugged myself, but I couldn't stop the violent shivers.

I turned away from the mirror, gasping, struggling to force away the icy chill.

I don't believe it. I drank more of the stuff.

Now I'll probably be invisible for the rest of my life.

The shivers stopped as quickly as they had started. I took one last frantic look into the mirror. No sign of me. Then I picked up the bottle of formula and shoved it into my jacket pocket. Maybe someone could figure out what was in this stuff.

I stepped out of the dressing room. My mind was whirring. My whole body felt heavy, heavy with disappointment—and fear.

I stepped out onto the sidewalk, lowered my head, and started to run full speed. I didn't think about where I was going. I didn't even see where I was headed. Cars and people and stores flew past me in a dizzying whirl of color.

I let out a hoarse cry. I couldn't keep my frustration inside.

Two teenage girls getting into a car turned to see who made that howl. I watched the confusion on their faces when they didn't see anyone around.

I had my eyes on them. I didn't realize I'd been running in the street, along the curb. I smashed headfirst into a parked car. Blinding pain roared down my whole body. I didn't move. Just threw myself onto the trunk of the car and waited for the pain to fade.

"Hey—! Who did that?" A man was sitting in the front passenger seat. He whirled to the window. Of course, he couldn't see me.

I started to run again. I finally slowed to a walk when I reached the park. I was panting hard. My body was drenched in sweat.

Clouds covered the late afternoon sky. The sun had faded behind them, and the air grew heavy, as if it was about to rain.

I walked along the wide path that led through the park. My house was not far from the other side of the park. Walking slowly, I started to calm down a little. The waves of anger had stopped, and I began to feel weary. Exhausted. After running for miles, my legs felt as if they each weighed a thousand pounds.

I was halfway through the park when I heard the scrape of footsteps behind me. I turned. No one there.

I continued walking. Still heard the footsteps, soft but steady. Close behind me.

I stopped and turned again. I squinted into the gray light. No one behind me. No one on the path.

I turned to walk again. And someone grabbed me by the shoulders.

"Hey! Let go!" I cried. "Let *go* of me!"

I spun around.

There was no one there.

Oh, yes there was.

Of course. It had to be Marvin.

Finally, I had help!

28

"Frankie, it's me." The hands loosened on my shoulders.

I stumbled back a step.

"It's me. Mystical Marvin," he said. "I followed you from the theater."

"I knew it was you," I said. "Where have you been?"

"Here and there," he said.

We were alone in the park, two invisible people. "Make me normal again," I said. "Please. Hurry. Make me normal, okay?"

Silence for a long moment. Then he replied, "I can't."

"What do you *mean*?" I cried. "You have to. You have to bring me back. You're the only one—"

"I can't," he said again. "I'm stuck, too, Frankie."

"But—but—!" I sputtered.

"No," he answered in a whisper. "I . . . I must have mixed the formula wrong. I thought I followed the sorcerer's instructions. But I must have made it too strong or something. It worked a couple of times, and then it didn't. I definitely made a mistake."

I suddenly had a heavy feeling in the pit of my stomach. As if I'd swallowed a bowling ball. "You really can't help me?" I said, my voice cracking.

"I can't."

"But . . . how long will this last?" I demanded.

Another long pause. I watched a squirrel run across the path. It hopped onto a park bench, rose up on its back legs, and appeared to be watching us. But, of course, it couldn't be.

"I don't know how long it will last," Mystical Marvin said finally. "Maybe a long time. Maybe *forever.*"

29

In school the next day, no one knew I was there.

That was fine with me. I didn't feel like talking with anyone anyway. And since I was invisible, there wasn't much I could do in class without freaking everyone out and causing a riot.

At lunchtime, Melody, Eduardo, and Ari were huddled at a table at the back of the lunchroom. I was about to pull out a chair and let them know I was there with them.

But then I realized they were talking about me and about our magic club. So I stood at the edge of the table and listened.

"We can still have the club without Frankie," Melody was saying. "It won't be the same. But maybe we can find some new kids to join."

"Yeah. Fun," Eduardo agreed.

My friends want to forget about me and have the club without me?

A stab of anger hurt my chest.

Ari leaned over the table toward Melody and

Eduardo across from him. "I have to tell you something I never told anyone," he said in a low voice.

"What's that?" Melody asked.

Ari had a strange grin on his face. A guilty grin. "Remember at the assembly when Frankie was doing the levitation trick? I deliberately dropped him. It wasn't an accident."

Melody gasped. Eduardo just stared at him.

"Ari—why?" Melody demanded.

Ari shrugged. His grin grew wider. "I just thought it would be funnier."

Funnier?

I waited for my friends to get angry. To tell Ari he couldn't be in the club anymore.

But Melody just said, "Ari, it wasn't very funny."

And that was that. They started talking about other kids who might join the club. And they talked about new tricks they wanted to learn.

I sat there staring at my friends, feeling my anger build.

I knew Ari was a creep. But I really thought Eduardo and Melody would stand up for me.

And I never dreamed they'd want to continue the magic club without me.

Okay, I thought. *Okay, I get it. I see what kind of friends you are.*

Let's see how well you do when YOU disappear forever!

30

Before the next magic club meeting, I sneaked down to Ari's basement before my three friends arrived for their club meeting.

Buster, Ari's big dog, had been sleeping in a square of sunlight by the high window. But he sat up, alert, when I entered the rec room.

"Hey, Buster," I whispered. "You can sense that I'm here—can't you?"

The fur on his back stood on end. He lowered his head and made loud breathing sounds.

I didn't have any time to waste. I saw that Mrs. Goodwyn had already set the lemonade pitcher down on the table along with a tray of oatmeal cookies. There were three glasses beside the pitcher.

I removed the little bottle of disappearing formula from my jacket pocket. And I poured a small amount of the yellow liquid into each glass. Then I filled the glasses with lemonade.

All ready. A nice surprise for the three traitors.

I paced back and forth as I waited for them to

arrive. Was I excited? For sure. Finally, a little payback.

A few minutes later, the three of them appeared. Eduardo carried his large magic kit. He set it down right in front of me.

Ari was waving a magic wand. "I have some awesome new ideas for tricks," he said.

"Me too," Melody said.

They had no idea I was standing there watching them. Only Buster had a clue. Buster kept his eyes on me, as if he could see me.

"Let's eat first," Eduardo said. "I'm hungry. I couldn't eat that stuff they had for lunch this afternoon."

"Yeah. What *was* that?" Ari said. "It wasn't real meat, was it?"

"I think it was dog food!" Melody said.

They turned to Buster. He kept his eyes on me. The dog paid no attention to them.

They sat down at the table. My heart started to pound.

Just a few seconds now, and they'll have their surprise.

My usual chair was empty. I carefully slid into it. I wanted to watch this close-up.

Eduardo grabbed for a cookie. All three of them began to devour cookies.

"Too bad about Frankie," Eduardo said.

"Yeah. Too bad," Ari echoed. He reached for one of the lemonade glasses.

That's when Buster decided to move.

The big dog jumped onto my chair. Actually, he leaped onto my lap.

He knew. He knew I was there. Maybe he smelled me. I don't know.

But he went into his old routine. Licking my face with his fat tongue. Licking me. Furiously licking my face.

I tried to push Buster off me. But I saw Melody's expression change. And then all three of them let out startled shouts.

"Frankie? You're back!" Melody shouted.

The big dog kept licking my face.

"I—I can see you!" Eduardo cried.

"Your face—!" Ari pointed.

"Huh?" My brain spun in confusion. Could they really see me?

I raised my right hand. Buster lowered his head and licked my hand.

My hand instantly came back into view.

"I don't believe it!" I cried. "Buster is bringing me back! Dog saliva is the antidote. Dog saliva is the answer!"

"My dog is a hero!" Ari proclaimed. "Yay for Buster!"

"I'm back. I'm back." I just kept repeating the words. I was so happy. I let Buster lick away.

I was back. I didn't need revenge anymore.

I hugged the big dog as he licked my neck.

"A toast to Buster!" Ari exclaimed. He raised

his lemonade glass high. Melody and Eduardo raised their glasses, too. "To Buster!" they shouted.

"No! Wait—!" I cried. "Wait! Please—!"

"Cheers!" Ari said.

And I watched all three of them drink their glasses down and disappear.

EPILOGUE FROM SLAPPY

Hahaha. I know why Frankie didn't try harder to save his friends. He wanted all the oatmeal cookies for himself!

You know, it's no fun performing tricks if your audience is invisible! The kids should forget about magic. Now they can have some really awesome hide-and-seek games! Hahahaha.

Well, time for me to vanish. But I'll reappear before you can say *abracadabra*, with another scary Goosebumps story.

Remember, this is *SlappyWorld*.

You only *scream* in it!

SLAPPYWORLD #4:
PLEASE DO NOT FEED THE WEIRDO

Read on for a preview!

SLAPPY HERE, EVERYONE.

Welcome to *SlappyWorld*.

Yes, it's Slappy's world—You're only *screaming* in it! Hahaha.

Readers Beware: Don't call me a dummy, Dummy. I'm so smart, I can spell IQ forward *and* backward! Ha. I'm so bright, I use my own head as a night-light!

I'm handsome, too. I'm so good-looking, when I look in a mirror, the mirror says, "Thank you!" Hahaha.

I'm so handsome, I win an award just for waking up in the morning! Haha!

(I know that doesn't make any sense. But, hey, slave, who's going to be *brave* enough to tell me that?)

I'm generous, too. I like to share. I like to share *scary stories* to make you scream and shake all over. I don't want to give you a nightmare, slave. I want *your whole life* to be a nightmare! Hahahaha!

Here's a story that's a real scream. It's about a brother and sister named Jordan and Karla. They have a lot of fun at a carnival—until an ugly monster decides to have fun with *them*!

You're not afraid of ugly monsters—*are* you? Then go ahead. Start the story. I call it ***Please Do Not Feed the Weirdo.***

It's just one more tale from *SlappyWorld*!

1

I took a big bite of the fluffy blue candy. I could feel the powdery sugar stick to my face.

Karla pointed to the cone in my hand. "Jordan, you have a spider in your cotton candy," she said.

I let out a loud "ULLLLLLP!" and the cone went flying into the air. I watched it land with a soft *plop* onto the pavement.

Karla tossed back her head and laughed. "You're too easy!"

Mom shook her head. "Karla, why are you always scaring your brother?"

She grinned. "Because it's fun?"

Grumbling to myself, I bent down and picked the cotton candy off the ground. Some of the blue stuff stuck to my sneakers. I took another bite anyway.

Some kids like to be scared and some don't. And I totally don't. I saw the Tunnel of Fear up ahead, and I knew Karla would force me to go in there with her.

My name is Jordan Keppler, and I'm twelve, a year older than Karla. I don't like to brag, but ... I get better grades than Karla, and I'm better at sports than Karla, and I have more friends than Karla does.

So just because she likes scary things doesn't make her any kind of big deal.

I looked all around. Carnival World was crowded because it was a beautiful spring night. I saw dozens of kids on the boardwalk, going from the game booths to the rides. And I knew a lot of them were walking right *past* the Tunnel of Fear because they were like me.

What's the fun of screaming your head off, anyway?

I tossed my cotton candy cone in a trash can. "Where's that ride with the swings that go really high?" I asked.

"You mean that baby ride in the kiddie park?" Karla said.

Dad leaned over and took a big bite of Karla's cotton candy. "If you two want to go into the Tunnel of Fear, Mom and I will wait here," he said.

"No thanks," I said. "I'll wait out here, too."

Karla pressed her hands against her waist and tossed back her curly red hair. "Well, I'm not going in alone, Jerkface."

"Don't call your brother names," Mom said.

"I didn't," Karla replied. "That *is* his name." She thinks she's so smart and funny.

"Don't make your sister go in there alone," Dad said. He put his hands on my shoulders. "Jordan, you're not scared, are you?"

He *knew* I was scared. Why bother to ask?

"Of *course* I'm not scared," I said. "It's just that . . . I ate all that cotton candy. I have to sit down and digest it."

I know. I know. That was lame. You don't have to tell me.

Karla grabbed my hand and tugged me hard toward the entrance. "Come on, Jordan. We don't come to the carnival very often. We have to do *everything.*"

I turned back to Mom and Dad. They were both making shooing motions with their hands. They were no help at all.

Don't get me wrong. I love Carnival World. I love the dart games and the corn dogs on a stick and the Ferris wheel and the Dunk-the-Clown water tank.

There are only two things I don't love. The rollercoaster rides that make you go upside down. And the Tunnel of Fear. And somehow—thanks to my sister—I knew I had both of those in my *near* future.

Karla and I walked up the wooden ramp to the tunnel entrance. "See you later!" I heard Mom shout. "If you survive!"

Ha. She and Karla have the same sick sense of humor.

Purple and red lights flashed all around us, and I heard deep, evil laughter—horror-movie laughter—echoing inside the tunnel. And screams. Lots of shrill screams. I couldn't tell if they were recorded or if they were from real people inside the ride.

Karla gave the young guy at the entrance two tickets, and he motioned us to the open cars. They were moving slowly along a track toward the dark cave opening where the ride began.

She pushed me into a car and slid in beside me. "This is so cool," she gushed. "We should have brought a barf bag for you."

Ha again.

"It's all fake," I said. "It's all babyish scares. Too phony to be scary. Seriously."

Wish I had been right about that.

As we rolled into total blackness, the door on our moving car slammed shut. A safety bar dropped down over our legs.

The car spun quickly, then slid along an invisible track beneath us. I gripped the safety bar with both hands. My eyes squinted into the darkness. I couldn't see a thing—

—Until a grinning skull shot down from above. It stopped an inch from my face, and its jagged, broken teeth snapped up and down as shrill laughter floated out.

I gasped. I didn't scream. I gripped the safety bar a little tighter.

Something damp and sticky brushed my face. I raised both hands to swipe at it, to try to push it off me.

Beside me, Karla laughed. "Yucky cobwebs," she said. She poked me. "And you know if there are cobwebs, there has to be . . ."

She didn't need to say it. At least a dozen

rubbery, fat black spiders bounced over the car. I tried to brush them off my face, but there were too many of them.

The car spun again, and I stared into a wall of darkness. Were there other people in the tunnel? I couldn't see them and I couldn't hear them.

Karla screamed as a huge, caped vampire jumped into our car. *"I want to drink your bloooood!"* it exclaimed. The vampire lowered its fangs to Karla's neck—but then disappeared.

Karla shuddered. She grabbed my sleeve. "That was creepy."

"It's all computer graphics," I said. I was trying to be the brave one. But to be honest, my stomach was doing cartwheels and my throat was suddenly as dry as the cotton candy.

Then evil cackling surrounded our car, and we jolted to a stop. I rocked against the safety bar, then bounced back.

The cackling stopped.

Silence.

I heard a high-pitched scream. A girl's scream that echoed off the tunnel walls.

We sat in solid darkness. My heart started to pound.

"Think there's something wrong?" I whispered. My hands were suddenly cold and sweaty on the safety bar.

"We definitely stalled," Karla said. "Unless maybe this is all part of the ride. You know. An extra-thrill part." Typical Karla. Now she didn't sound scared at all.

My heart was pounding. "It'll probably start back up, right?"

"For sure," she said.

So we waited. Waited and listened. Listened to the heavy silence.

No voices or music or sounds from the carnival on the other side of the walls. The only thing I could hear was the throb of blood pulsing in my ears.

We waited some more.

"Cold in here," Karla murmured. "Like a tomb." She hugged herself.

"You don't think that girl's scream was a real scream—do you?" I whispered. My skin prickled.

"Why doesn't the ride start up again?" Karla whispered back, ignoring my question.

"Why are we whispering?" I asked.

Even our whispers echoed in the black tunnel.

I spread my hand over my chest. I could feel my fluttering heartbeat. I had tried to be brave. But . . . I knew I was about to lose it.

I could feel a scream forming in my throat. Feel all my muscles tighten. Feel the panic creeping up from my stomach.

How long had we been waiting in the cold, silent darkness? Ten minutes? Fifteen? More?

I gripped the safety bar so hard my hands

ached. "Hey!" I shouted. "Is anyone *else* in here? Can anyone hear me? Hey!"

No answer. No one.

"I think we're the only car in here," Karla said. "Creepy, huh?"

"Can anyone hear me?" I shouted again, my voice high and shrill. "Who is in here with us? Anyone here?"

Silence.

"Hey! We need help—"

I couldn't finish my cry. Fingers wrapped around my neck from behind. Cold, bone-hard fingers . . . tightening . . . tightening. I tried to scream. But the fingers were so tight, I couldn't make a sound!

About the Author

R.L. Stine says he gets to scare people all over the world. So far, his books have sold more than 400 million copies, making him one of the most popular children's authors in history. The Goosebumps series has more than 150 titles and has inspired a TV series and two motion pictures. R.L. himself is a character in the movies! He has also written the teen series Fear Street, and the Mostly Ghostly and Nightmare Room series. He is currently writing a series of graphic novels entitled Just Beyond. R.L. Stine lives in New York City with his wife, Jane, an editor and publisher. You can learn more about him at rlstine.com

REVENGE OF THE LIVING DUMMY
R.L. STINE
SCHOLASTIC

CREEP FROM THE DEEP
R.L. STINE
SCHOLASTIC

MONSTER BLOOD FOR BREAKFAST!
R.L. STINE
SCHOLASTIC

THE SCREAM OF THE HAUNTED MASK
R.L. STINE
SCHOLASTIC

DR. MANIAC VS. ROBBY SCHWARTZ
R.L. STINE
SCHOLASTIC

WHO'S YOUR MUMMY?
R.L. STINE
SCHOLASTIC

MY FRIENDS CALL ME MONSTER
R.L. STINE
SCHOLASTIC

SAY CHEESE - AND DIE SCREAMING!
R.L. STINE
SCHOLASTIC

WELCOME TO CAMP SLITHER
R.L. STINE
SCHOLASTIC

SCHOLASTIC

www.scholastic.com/goosebumps

GBHL19H2

THE SCARIEST PLACE ON EARTH!

Goosebumps HorrorLand
HELP! WE HAVE STRANGE POWERS!
R.L. STINE
SCHOLASTIC

Goosebumps HorrorLand
ESCAPE FROM HORRORLAND
R.L. STINE
SCHOLASTIC

Goosebumps HorrorLand
THE STREETS OF PANIC PARK
R.L. STINE
SCHOLASTIC

Goosebumps HorrorLand
WHEN THE GHOST DOG HOWLS
R.L. STINE
SCHOLASTIC

Goosebumps HorrorLand
LITTLE SHOP OF HAMSTERS
R.L. STINE
SCHOLASTIC

Goosebumps HorrorLand
HEADS, YOU LOSE!
R.L. STINE
SCHOLASTIC

Goosebumps HorrorLand
WEIRDO HALLOWEEN
R.L. STINE
SCHOLASTIC

Goosebumps HorrorLand
THE WIZARD OF OOZE
R.L. STINE
SCHOLASTIC

Goosebumps HorrorLand
SLAPPY NEW YEAR!
R.L. STINE
SCHOLASTIC

Goosebumps HorrorLand
THE HORROR AT CHILLER HOUSE
R.L. STINE
SCHOLASTIC

HALL OF HORRORS—HALL OF FAME FOR THE TRULY TERRIFYING!

Goosebumps HALL OF HORRORS
CLAWS!
R.L. STINE
SCHOLASTIC

Goosebumps HALL OF HORRORS
NIGHT OF THE GIANT EVERYTHING
R.L. STINE
SCHOLASTIC

SCHOLASTIC

www.scholastic.com/goosebumps

SCHOLASTIC and associated logos
trademarks and/or registered
demarks of Scholastic Inc.

GBHL19H2

R. L. Stine's Fright Fest!
Now with Splat Stats and More!

Goosebumps
THE WEREWOLF of FEVER SWAMP
R.L. STINE

Goosebumps
A NIGHT in TERROR TOWER
R.L. STINE

Goosebumps
WELCOME to DEAD HOUSE
R.L. STINE

Goosebumps
WELCOME to CAMP NIGHTMARE
R.L. STINE

Goosebumps
GHOST BEACH
R.L. STINE

Goosebumps
The SCARECROW WALKS at MIDNIGHT
R.L. STINE

Goosebumps
YOU CAN'T SCARE ME!
R.L. STINE

Goosebumps
RETURN OF THE MUMMY
R.L. STINE

Goosebumps
REVENGE of the LAWN GNOMES
R.L. STINE

Goosebumps
PHANTOM OF THE AUDITORIUM
R.L. STINE

Goosebumps
VAMPIRE BREATH
R.L. STINE

Goosebumps
STAY OUT of the BASEMENT
R.L. STINE

Goosebumps SlappyWorld

THIS IS SLAPPY'S WORLD—
YOU ONLY SCREAM IN IT!

I AM SLAPPY'S EVIL TWIN
R.L. STINE

ATTACK OF THE JACK!
R.L. STINE

SLAPPY BIRTHDAY TO YOU
R.L. STINE

PLEASE DO NOT
FEED THE WEIRDO
R.L. STINE

ESCAPE FROM
SHUDDER MANSION
R.L. STINE

THE DUMMY MEETS THE MUMMY!
R.L. STINE

THE GHOST OF SLAPPY
R.L. STINE

IT'S ALIVE! IT'S ALIVE!
R.L. STINE

REVENGE OF
THE INVISIBLE BOY!
R.L. STINE

DIARY OF A DUMMY
R.L. STINE

31901065211403

SCHOLASTIC

GBSLAPPYWORLD10